Heart of Fire

Winchester Brothers Book 2

Copyright 2015 Melissa Barker-Simpson

All rights reserved. No part of this publication may be reproduced, distributed, or transmitted in any form or by any means, including photocopying, recording, or other electronic or mechanical methods without the prior written permission of the publisher, except in the case of brief quotations embodied in critical reviews and certain other non-commercial uses permitted by copyright law.

Preface

Tyler eased his foot off the accelerator, just a little. He felt the car protest. It was built for speed. He grinned, slow and easy. Life was good. At eighteen he didn't have a care in the world; no responsibilities, nothing to worry about except for which university to attend.

Convincing his father to buy him the sports car had been child's play. All it took was reference to his brother's absence and his genuine envy that Sebastian was out in the big wide world. Tyler couldn't imagine leaving Winchester long term, but the thought of losing another son had kept his father sweet.

He felt invincible; young, smart and sophisticated in the flame-red Porsche. The road stretched ahead, enticing him to open her up - to give the beautiful beast free rein. He couldn't have known what was around the corner.

Tyler sensed the commotion before he saw it. Some impending doom, or perhaps an echo of the disaster ahead. He noticed the fire first. It demanded attention as it mushroomed outward, threatening everything in its path. Heat came second. Even from the opposite side of the carriageway, separated by the central reservation, it was enough to incite fear.

His brain froze, stuttering in its attempt to process the scene. The twisted, burning metal of a dozen vehicles too horrific to contemplate. As he edged closer he hit a wall of sound. It was like a physical blow, and it snapped him out of his stupor in time to prevent another collision. Slamming on the breaks he stopped a hairs breadth from the car in front. He knew what had caused the tail back; the carnage across from them was hypnotizing.

Flipping his indicator, he checked his mirror and pulled over. His wasn't the only car to hug the hard shoulder. A small group gathered at the front of a dark blue Range Rover, all talking frantically into a series of devices.

He stepped onto the road, his eyes drawn to the wreckage opposite. Without the insulation of his car he could hear the piercing screams of those trapped. The sound shot straight through his heart, sending another ripple of fear through him. He wanted to stay and fight for these people, as much as he wanted to get back in the Porsche and leave the nightmare behind.

A siren cut through the chaos, and all but Tyler turned towards the sound. His gaze followed the sea of cars, all the way back to the ball of heat he could feel like a brand against his cheek. He made a quick calculation and estimated there were twenty cars surrounding the crash site. It felt natural to follow the small group as they headed towards the central reservation. They were the only line of defence until the firefighters arrived.

He climbed into the danger zone, thinking only of the desperate cries of those trapped. His heart pumped adrenalin around his body so fast that, at first, he didn't react when the explosions started.

The fire devoured everything it touched, heating it up so quickly that tyres popped under the pressure. The screaming intensified and it was like a call in his blood, a call to action, and he followed it without question. The fire called to him too. He watched in both horror and fascination as it continued its domination.

He was almost upon the first vehicle when a fire fighter stepped into his path and told him to stay back. Tyler couldn't decide if it was the stubborn look in his own eyes, or the sheer desperation in the officer's, which helped them make the choice.

As Tyler went one way, the fire-fighter went the other. They were on a quest to save lives and only one of them was qualified.

His intended destination, a Ford Focus, was sandwiched between two larger models. The driver on the left lay slumped over the steering wheel. On the right, a young man talked frantically on his phone. After a moment's indecision, he snapped his attention back to the Focus and a young child's terrified wailing. The pitch was so high he had to repress the urge to cover his ears.

He ignored the startled glance from the phone wielding youth, climbed onto his bonnet and jumped across to the Ford. The driver, a woman in her earlier forties, lay unconscious behind the wheel. He squinted, his breath rushing out in relief when he saw the rise and fall of her chest.

Though it was difficult, his mind tuned out the cacophony of sound around him. He stepped onto the next car and jumped to the ground so he was on the passenger side of the left-hand car. Prying open the door he ducked inside. The male driver faced him, allowing Tyler a good look at the open face wound. Blood ran in a river down his cheek, making Tyler's stomach clench. He looked to be in his fifties, but it was hard to tell.

"Sir, can you hear me?" he called. Nothing. No response.

Taking a deep breath, he leaned in further and stretched out to feel for a pulse in the man's neck. For a long tense moment he thought the driver was dead – hearing nothing but the frantic beat of his own heart. Then he caught something, a weak flutter against his fingers. He was alive, though even as an amateur Tyler knew the danger.

Ducking back out, he turned in a circle and watched the activity around him. The professionals were on hand. "We need some help over here," he called, not expecting an immediate response.

"What have you got?" a female paramedic asked, jogging in his direction.

"Two unconscious drivers." He indicated the male driver with his thumb. "He's unresponsive and his pulse is thready."

He stepped back to give her room, his eyes wandering to the Focus. Two fire-fighters had the boot open and were working to calm the screaming infant.

He scanned the other cars, wondering for a moment why he was there, in the midst of all the chaos. With adrenalin leaking from his body, he registered the heat pushing against his skin. It was unbearable. He could hear the fire too. It wasn't something he could explain, even to himself. It just was. The beast was having fun and it wasn't about to give up without a fight.

"Sir, are you hurt?" a paramedic asked, shining a light into his eyes.

He cringed away instinctively. "No, I…I just wanted to help."

"We have things under control now. Why don't I get you to safety?"

Tyler nodded. "My car…" The words died in his throat when he caught a glint of yellow; a Volkswagen in the middle of the blaze. No, that couldn't be right. Other people were crazy enough to buy a canary-yellow Beetle. But he knew, even before he recognised the familiar dint in the bumper. For a moment he could only stare in horror as flames licked across the paint-work. And then her face worked its way into his mind and he lost it.

"Lilly-May," he shouted, his body coiling in readiness to run.

The paramedic pre-empted the move, placing a hand on his arm in warning. "Sir, I need you to come with me now."

Something dark rose up in Tyler, stealing all reason; perhaps even sanity. It took two firefighters to subdue him, and even then his mind was racing, trying to find a way to get past them.

"There's nothing you can do, son," the elder of the two said, his gentle voice grating along Tyler's nerves.

"You have to help her. She…" His breath rushed out as nausea clutched in his stomach. The scream hadn't been her, he told himself. She wasn't calling to him. "Please."

"We'll do everything we can." The same gentle voice, the same low burn of irritation along his skin. "Go get yourself checked out. We've got this."

They stared at each other until Tyler felt the heat burn his skin, like an urgent reminder of where they were. If he didn't allow the firefighters to do their job, it would be too late.

He nodded, watching the men run back into battle, because that's what it was - a battle. The fire a ferocious beast, seducing even as she punished. Such thoughts led to Lilly-May and he felt the panic rise again, his heart heavy with the need to save her. It was agony, waiting for the firefighters to douse the flames and contain the outbreak. His gaze never left the scene, his ears alert for any sign that she was okay.

When he heard mention of a passenger, a wave of ice travelled up his spine and his phone was in his hand before he'd even registered the thought.

Mind whirling, he tried to remember where his brother was supposed to be. "Come on, come on," he said, growing impatient with the ring tone.

"Hey, Ty."

The sound of her voice brought him to his knees. She was with Dylan. She wasn't in the car. "Oh God," he croaked, shuddering. "I thought you were in the car."

There was a long, tense silence. "Tyler, what is it? What about my car?"

He was aware of the police officer now, bent on one knee, talking to him. Heard Lilly-May calling to him, asking what was wrong. Her rising panic mingled with the scene around him and he closed his eyes a moment - closed his mind to it all.

When he spoke again, his voice was deadly calm. "There's been an accident on the M3." He swallowed. "Who's in your car, Lilly?"

"My parents." It came out in a hushed whisper. "I've been having a few problems with it and Mum persuaded Dad to take it for a spin. You know how she worries…oh God. This is my fault. What happened Tyler…you have to tell me what happened."

"Tyler? What's going on?" It was his brother's voice now.

"A major pile-up on the M3. It's bad, Dylan. Her car…" He glanced towards it. "It's bad," he said again.

"Are you injured?" Concern replaced his brother's irritation.

"No. I wasn't involved. I stopped…" A wall of flame shot into the air, choking the words in his throat.

Was it wrong he wondered, to see the beauty in it? The beast had unleashed her power, and the beat or two of silence was almost reverent. It rushed back in on a wave; the sound, the colour, the heat. Through it all, Tyler couldn't take his eyes from the battle. In that moment he knew. He had been claimed. This would be his role in life. To tame the dragon.

Chapter 1

The sounds of the emergency room exploded around Tyler, and yet he heard only one thing. Not the harried feet, the cacophony of machines, the barked out orders, or chatter of the wounded. No, Tyler was in a vacuum and everything centred on the flat, haunting tone of his friend's heart monitor. Grayson had lost his fight, and there was nothing Tyler or anyone else could do about it.

He felt his grief swell out of control; an explosion which seared across his chest, burned up his throat, and made him want to roar with the intensity of it. He wasn't embarrassed by the sheen of tears as he looked through the panel of glass at his friend. His body was torn and broken, but there were no burns along his skin. He had been the best firefighter Tyler knew, and yet it seemed unjust he had lost his life in the line of duty without a mark. Grayson often joked that fire was the only woman he courted, and Tyler had a strange thought that she felt cheated too.

He felt a hand settle on his shoulder and steeled himself for the consolation.
"I'm sorry, man. I know you guys were close."

Tyler tore his gaze from the scene behind the glass and turned to Michaels, a senior member of their team. As their eyes met he thought of their other fallen comrade.

"Daniel?" he asked. It was the only word he could form, his throat was so raw.

"Still in surgery." Michaels' eyes dropped to Tyler's arm. "I'm glad to see you finally got that stitched up."

The emotion swelled again at the sight of his brothers in arms, gathered silently around them. There were a few missing, but Tyler knew they would be with Daniel and his family, showing their support.

"I have to go," he mumbled, and hightailed it out before a doctor could tell them what they already knew. They had lost a good man today.

He walked with no real destination in mind. His belongings were back at the station, so he didn't even have his house keys. He didn't care. There was nobody he wanted to see. No one he wanted to call.

He was blind to the hustle and bustle of life in the town centre, barely noticed the tourists as they stopped to admire the sights and sounds of Winchester. It was home to him, the only home he'd ever known, but right then it felt empty.

It was growing dark before he figured out which way his feet were taking him. The place he always went when he needed to recharge and regroup. As he walked the long drive towards his parents' house, the ache in his chest grew. He couldn't hide his hurts from his mother, and maybe that was the point.

She was in the kitchen where he'd known she would be. Veronica Davies wasn't opposed to help, and had no choice considering her busy schedule, but his mother rarely shared her kitchen. It was her domain; her pride and joy.

He watched her for a moment, peering through the window as he'd done at the hospital, only this was a far different scene. The room before him exploded with colour, from the black and yellow units to the fresh, home-grown vegetables scattered across one of the surfaces. There were tulips, their yellow heads drooping a little in the heat; a large basket of fruit; a fridge covered in postcards from across the globe and his mother, trim and elegant in one of her housecoats. It should have brought him comfort, and yet all he saw were the contrasts. Grayson's resting place had been sterile and cold, devoid of life or hope.

He saw a flicker of colour and turned towards it, stomach clenching when she stepped into the room, the woman he'd loved his whole life - Lilly-May. Her burnt orange coat was like the heart of a flame, casting him back to the warehouse fire and the scene when they'd first arrived. To banish the image, he concentrated on her face. Sometimes it hurt just to look at her, knowing she could never be his. Her pale blonde hair was swept back and though he couldn't see it, he knew it was held in a sleek knot, one he'd dreamt of unravelling. She was slim and petite, and side by side she barely reached his breast bone. But she had always been larger than life. The flame to the beating heart of him. With her dark green eyes and wide, generous mouth, he had been captivated with her before he knew what it was to want.

Now he longed to sink himself into her arms, to breathe in the sweet scent of strawberries and cream; it was how she always smelled to him. The memory of it forced air into his lungs, so he could no longer smell the cloying aroma of smoke, and instead of the sirens playing in his head, he heard the sweet sound of her laughter.

He ducked back when her head came up, as though she had sensed his presence. He couldn't face her. Not now. She made him want, and he had no right to want.

Walking to the side of the house he ducked into the shadows, as the back door swung open.

"I'll come by after work on Thursday and we can finalise the plans," Lilly-May said, her voice as gentle as the breeze.

There was a brief silence before his mother spoke. "Drive safe, sweetheart."

Tyler dropped his head back against the wall and waited until it was safe to come out. He wondered briefly why Lilly-May hadn't used the front entrance, since she had clearly parked on the other side of the house. When he ducked his head around the corner and saw her disappearing into the patch of trees on his parents' property, he got his answer. She was headed to where his father had found her almost twenty-two years ago, on a cold October evening when she had run away from home and wandered onto their land.

Part of him wanted to go to her, and he would have, except he had his own demons to fight. This night wasn't about him, or his distraction with Lilly-May, it was about his friend. He shouldn't have come here, should still be at the hospital, but couldn't make his legs move. Sinking to the ground, he pulled his coat around him and allowed himself to rest for a while.

It didn't do any good. When he stopped, he remembered the sound of falling timber and crushed bone. He thought about the weight on his chest, and the time he'd wasted trying to free himself from the rubble, while his friend lay dying.

Grayson wouldn't give in to self-pity. Grayson would be rallying the team, and using their strength to push through the loss. It was enough to get him onto his feet, though he waited several long minutes before retracing his steps to the back door. Once there he hovered, one hand on the frame and the other clenched at his side as he tried to pull back the worst of his grief.

His mother looked up when he entered, and the moment she saw his face, she stopped what she was doing to pull out a chair at the kitchen counter.

"Sit," she said. It was the first time he'd seen her look anything but confident.

He did as she asked, wanting to sooth as much as be soothed. But when she waited for him to speak he couldn't find the reassurance she was looking for. Instead, he concentrated on the familiar aroma of roasted chicken and allowed the warmth of the room to wash over him. On any other day he would have taken over the task his mother had abandoned, cutting the vegetables waiting on the chopping board. But then, if this had been a normal day, his mother would still be preparing the meal while they caught up on their news.

She walked over to the fridge and took out a jug of milk. With practiced ease she poured it into a pan on the stove and reached into the long cupboard on her right. She was bringing out the big guns, he realised, and making him her signature hot chocolate. His eyes burned with unshed tears. It was her way of taking care of him, and she had been making the smooth, frothy concoction since the first time he'd taken a tumble and scraped his knee. His hurts were harder to fix, but the gesture soothed, as did her love.

Having prepared the ingredients she returned to him and stood beside the chair. "Do you want to talk about it?" she asked, stroking his hair.

Tyler's throat squeezed shut and he could only shake his head.

"That's okay," she murmured, wrapping her arms around him. "I'm glad you came."

He closed his eyes and took her comfort, if only for a moment. He didn't speak until he could trust his voice. "Can I stay in the cottage for a while?"

She stepped back to look into his face. "Why don't I bring the drink across?"

He nodded again, touched by the simple understanding. She always knew what he needed.

"I'm here when you want to talk about it," she said, leaning to kiss him on the cheek. "Take all the time you need."

Tyler watched her for a few more moments, needing the simple light of family before he was swallowed up by the grief burning a hole in his chest.

His mother didn't say anything when he stood to leave. She handed him the key to the cottage, a building which backed onto the main house, and resumed her task.

As he walked out into the cold night air, he thought of Daniel and felt a twinge of guilt. He was a coward for running out on his family at the hospital. He just didn't have the strength to lose another friend.

The path to the cottage was lit by a hundred shining stars, hanging from the trees on either side. It was Dylan's idea; his brother had built the two-storey cottage and landscaped the grounds circling it as a gift to their parents. Inside, the decor was their mother's doing. She had provided a space for each of them because she enjoyed the thought of keeping her family close. The living room was designed with Tyler in mind, with a floor to ceiling shelving unit to house his DVD collection. The surround sound, flat-screen television came equipped with an array of gadgets. It was also perfect for their impromptu family gatherings and was the heart of the place.

Needing the sense of family, he wandered through to the kitchen. This area belonged to Chris and was a chef's treasure trove. Every surface gleamed, and it was easy to picture Chris cooking at the centre island as he barked out instructions to the rest of them. They had adopted Chris into their family the moment Tyler's eldest brother, Sebastian had brought him into their lives. The pair were best friends throughout childhood and that hadn't changed. They now shared a business, and in respecting Sebastian's needs, an office sat adjacent to the kitchen and was his to use whenever he stopped by. Upstairs, in addition to a room for each, was an art studio for Dylan. When their sister, Connie, decided on her perfect space, Dylan would make it happen.

Shrugging off his jacket, he hung it on the hook at the bottom of the stairs and climbed. He needed to wash off the dirt and grime, and relieve his stiff joints. He chose the first bathroom he came to; stepping out of his clothes as he crossed the cream tile, he dumped them on a chair.

He turned up the heat on the shower and pushed his face under the spray. The water was like hot tears on his skin, but it didn't relieve the pressure. The steam made it worse. He felt disorientated, pulled back into the nightmare at the warehouse, where the smoke had been so thick it suffocated.

Grayson's voice echoed around the cubicle, haunting him with the memory. *"It's like being in the bowels of hell."*

"Get used to it, because it's where you're headed," Daniel had said, slapping a hand on his tank.

"Not me, my friend. I get a ticket straight to the pearly gates." Grayson's laughter ricocheted in Tyler's head, taunting him.

He found himself murmuring his response, now completely lost to the memories they were all he could see. "Wherever the ultimate location, it won't be today. Let's get out of here."

But they hadn't gotten out, not all of them. As he lathered soap into his hands, he tried to push the echoes from his mind, but they kept coming, and coming until he turned the temperature to freezing in a desperate attempt to stop the tirade. It was like a slap, one which cleared his mind so quickly, the reality of what had happened almost brought him to his knees. He gritted his teeth and stood under the brutal flow of cold water, punishing himself, though he had no idea why. By the time he turned the shower off, his aches were bone deep and he welcomed the pain.

He towelled himself dry, went to the hamper and flipped through for a pair of jeans in his size. The only sweatshirt he could find was in Dylan's, but it hardly mattered. He couldn't drum up the energy to care.

With his mind still on Daniel, he retraced his steps to the phone and called his Watch Manager.

"It's Tyler, sir - I'm calling-"

"I know why you're calling, son. Where are you?"

He swallowed the lump in his throat. He heard only concern in his commander's tone, and didn't deserve it. "I had to get out. I'm fine. I just couldn't watch another…is there any news on Daniel?"

"He's out of surgery, so all we can do now is wait. I'll call you on this number as soon as I have an update."

"Thank you, sir."

He dropped the receiver into its cradle before he did something stupid, like blubbered down the phone. Then he almost did when he saw the hot chocolate on a coaster on the coffee table. Moving to sit on the sofa he picked up the cup and felt the heat penetrate his cold skin. When he brought it to his lips he drew in the rich flavour of cocoa beans and thought of the gift of family.

Chapter 2

Lilly-May climbed out of the car and looked toward the welcome lights of the Davies household. In all the ways that counted, this was her home, but that hadn't always been the case. Perhaps she was feeling sentimental, a reaction to her impending birthday celebrations. She would be thirty in two days and her family were playing on her mind. It was why she was drawn to the spot where she had first met Simon and Veronica Davies, a day which had changed the course of her life.

She wandered through the small copse of trees bordering the property, thinking about the girl she had been. Her memories had changed over the years, were distorted by time, but then she had a woman's perspective now. Without the innocence of childhood, she understood the sacrifices her mother had made and no longer resented her.

She was five when she learned of her mother's unhappiness. She didn't understand why her mother cried, only that she was sad. Later she discovered the storm could last for hours, especially after a bitter argument. It usually ended with her father storming out of the house, and her mother dissolving into angry, bitter tears.

It terrified her, the cruel words they threw at each other. They grew more verbal as time went on, and more physical. By the time she was six, she understood that the escalation meant only one thing: they would hurt each other with more than their words. So she found a way to distract them; to control the increasingly violent outbursts.

Looking back she realised how significant her childish intervention had been. She could see them clearly, even after all these years. It still hurt that they had been so wrapped up in their own misery they couldn't see her pain.

Something broke in her that fateful night twenty years ago, something she couldn't get back. The memory was too strong to fight, so she closed her eyes and saw what her mind wanted her to see. It was like watching a scene from someone else's life, but she knew it wasn't – the agony was all hers.

Her parents had been particularly cruel that night. They argued with such vitriol that they barely noticed the child standing between them. Until the unforeseen happened. Until she opened her lungs and screamed so long and loud she was hoarse for days.

She couldn't remember if one of them reached for her. She had no memory of anything until she awoke on soft grass, amidst tall trees, dirty and exhausted.

The fear of not knowing where she was, or what had happened, outweighed everything else. So when a tall, dark-haired man stepped out of the shadows, the only thing she could do was stare at him.

"Hey. There now. I'm not going to hurt you," he said, in a voice that rumbled like thunder. "What are you doing out here in the middle of the night?"

Her response was a croak. It was the only sound she could make.

"Okay, that's okay." He glanced around as though seeking inspiration from the foliage. "We need to get you inside. It's freezing out here." He approached her the way he might a small cub. "Will you come with me? Let's go inside and we can figure this out."

Lilly-May blinked up at him. She wanted to curl into a ball and make herself invisible. She wanted her mother. That thought brought tears and the man jumped back as though he'd been bitten.

"Simon? Simon where are you?"

The new voice was soft in comparison to the man's; gentler. Lilly-May was drawn to it, though she couldn't have said why.

"Over here," he called.

She appeared a moment later, with a toddler attached to her hip. The boy had a mop of dark hair and sleepy blue eyes. They lit with interest when he saw her. The woman stopped, surprise and concern flickering across her face. She handed the boy to his father and crouched in front of her. "Hey there, sweetie. Are you hurt?" she asked.

Lilly-May shook her head, responding to her kind tone.

"Do you know where you are?"

She shook her head again, distracted by the boy fidgeting in his father's arms. Simon let him go, but kept a hand on his shoulder.

"Where did you come from?" the boy asked, with a hint of wonder.

"That's something we need to figure out," his mother said. "Why don't we go into the house and I'll get you a blanket. You must be cold."

Lilly-May looked from one to the other and tried to figure out what she should do.

The boy ducked out of his father's grasp and knelt beside his mother. "I'm Tyler," he said, holding out a hand. "It'll be okay. I'll take care of you."

She smiled at his words, at the serious light in his eyes. He was younger than she was, perhaps by three years, but she trusted him. Which was why she reached out and put her small hand in his.

And now, after twenty years, she still trusted him. He was one of the smartest people she knew, and the most compassionate. It wasn't something she'd ever put into words, but he had given her exactly what she needed that night: friendship. It didn't matter who she was, or where she came from. The Davies family had reunited her with her parents, and though the incident hadn't been the last of her family's troubles, they became the one constant in her life. A chance encounter, born from the desperation of a child, had changed everything. There was no way any of them could have foreseen that.

Shaking off the memory, she walked back towards the house. Veronica was expecting her, and she had dallied long enough.

She entered the kitchen and knew something was wrong. For one it was unusual to see Chris so early in the evening. He took his responsibilities at the restaurant too seriously. But what gave her pause were the deep grooves of worry under his eyes, a mirror image of Veronica's.

"What happened?" she asked, trying not to panic.

Veronica stepped forward to greet her. "It's Tyler. We were just discussing how best to help."

Lilly-May frowned as she accepted the hug. She knew about the fire, that he'd lost a member of his team, but Dylan had assured her he was okay. "What's going on, V?"

"You know how he is, how he thinks he can save everybody," Veronica said, on a long sigh. "It's the first time he's lost one of his own to a fire, and he's taking it pretty hard."

Chris walked over to the stove and took a pan from the heat. "He's holed himself up and we can't seem to get through to him," he said. "Grayson was a good friend."

His presence finally made sense when he began to pour chili into a bowl. It was Chris' version of comfort food. "Ty's here?"

He nodded. "In the cottage."

"Can I take it to him?" she asked, looking back at Veronica.

There was only the slightest hesitation. "He's not himself at the moment, Lilly. But I think he'd appreciate the gesture."

"Try to get him to eat some," Chris said, bringing a tray forward. "Most of it comes back untouched."

Veronica moved to open the back door for her. "Go easy on him. He isn't the best company right now."

Their concern made her nervous. Tyler was the strong one, the one they all went to for support, so she had no idea what to expect. She hadn't expected the complete absence of light at the cottage. Part of her wondered if the door would be locked, but when she balanced the tray on her hip and tried the handle, it turned.

The door led directly into the living room. It was a generous space with four large sofas, all facing a television, hung on the facing wall. She spotted Tyler immediately, stretched out on the second sofa. It was too dark to be sure, but he appeared to be staring at the ceiling.

"Provisions are here," she said, aiming for a lightness she didn't quite manage.

Tyler showed no surprise at the sound of her voice, but she saw how tense his body was, even in the dark. The shape of him was so familiar, she sensed the coiled power. His broad shoulders were the kind she thought could take on the world, but not today. This had her moving forward instinctively.

"Thank you," he said, in a voice which sounded rusty with disuse.

"I've had strict instructions to stay until you've eaten Chris' masterpiece," she told him, placing the tray onto the small coffee table. "If you're going to do that, we'll need a little light."

She walked over to one of the tall corner lamps and switched it on.

"I'll eat," he said, swinging his legs to the floor. "Thanks for stopping by, Lilly."

She turned to him, unperturbed by the rebuttal. His face was dark with shadows and he had yet to look at her. "I'm happy to help," she said, walking to the sofa and taking the seat beside him. "They're planning an intervention in there." She indicated the main house with a nod of her head. "Fair warning."

Finally, he turned and met her gaze. His eyes were so haunted she sucked in a shocked breath, she'd never seen them so dark. They were normally a crystal shade of blue, a colour he shared with his brothers. Tyler's were the most distinctive because they held so much light. It hurt to see the shadows in them now.

"I just need a little time. You'd be doing me a favour if you told them that."

When he broke eye contact, Lilly leaned forward to snag the bowl. "I'll gladly pass on your message, but you have to meet them halfway. Eat, Ty."

He looked down at the bowl, though he made no move to take it.

"If you eat half, I'll finish it off. That should give you another few hours at least."

His fingers closed around the bowl as his gaze met hers again. "Why are you here, Lilly?"

"Where else would I be? If I'd known you needed me, I'd have been here sooner." She rested her hand on top of his, still clutching the bowl. "You have to let someone in, Ty. I'm not saying it has to be me, but you can't bottle up your pain and expect us to sit by and watch."

His eyes fluttered shut as if heavy with fatigue. She'd never noticed how long his lashes were. They fanned out on his cheeks, not quite covering the bruises under his eyes.

"If you want me to leave, I'll hold them off as long as I can," she whispered, because she would have done anything right then to make it better.

"I don't want you to leave." He opened his eyes again and sat back against the sofa, taking the bowl. After a moment he raised the spoon and ate a mouthful of chili.

Lilly-May wanted to tell him how sorry she was about his friend, but she was afraid he would shut her out again, so she talked of the mundane. Each time he raised the spoon to his mouth, she felt a surge of relief, and continued to distract him with needless chatter.

"I actually stopped by to check on the plans for this weekend. Dylan only agreed to celebrate his thirtieth because I caved. It's a joint party." She eyed the bowl and saw he'd already eaten over half. "You do realise you made Chris' day now, right? He'll be bragging about his culinary magic for days."

"It'll be justified," Tyler said, leaning to put the bowl back on the tray. She was so surprised when he placed a cushion in her lap and laid his head on it, that for a moment she didn't know what to say. "It should have been me, Lilly," he whispered into the silence. "It should have been me."

She put a hand on his hair and ran her fingers through the soft dark waves in a soothing motion. "Tell me."

"We'd done our sweep and were on our way out," he began, his voice so quiet she had to concentrate to hear. "I was in front, heading the team, but I heard something and stopped to check it out. The fire was under control, but we were all wary of the structure and anxious to get out."

"So your friend walked ahead?"

Tyler nodded. "He made some joke about rats trying to push their way to the front and the next thing I knew the roof came down on our heads."

Her hand stilled in his hair as she digested the horror. "I'm so sorry, Ty."

He didn't say anything for a long time, so she continued to soothe and waited.

"I tried to get to him, but he had a beam pinning his chest and I couldn't shift it. Another of the guys was down, buried under a pile of rubble, so I cleared the way, praying help would arrive. Grayson was so quiet, and he never shuts up, not even for a minute, so it drove me crazy. I kept thinking it should have been me trapped under there."

"You can't know that, Tyler. It didn't happen because you weren't where you were supposed to be, or because you followed your instincts."

"Then why does it hurt so much?" he asked, making her heart ache.

"Because you lost a friend and you weren't ready to let go." She moved her hand to his shoulder and squeezed hard. "Let us help you, Ty. You don't have to go through this alone."

He fell quiet again, so long this time she thought he might be asleep.

"Will you stay a while?" he asked, his words drowsy.

"As long as you need," she promised, and dropped her head back against the sofa.

Chapter 3

Tyler felt a crushing weight on his chest. Something hard was pushing against his spine, and awareness returned like a blow. It was his tank. Panic struck as fast and lethal as a cobra. He couldn't catch his breath, felt sure he would suffocate in the dark. Fighting the steely grip of terror he pulled one of his arms free and pushed his mask aside. The air was acrid with dust and smoke, burning his lungs. A large piece of ceiling tile was covering the upper part of his body and he instinctively pushed against it. Nothing happened, which told him he was buried beneath part of the ceiling itself.

A fresh wave of anxiety clawed at him, squeezing his chest so the pressure was amplified.

Get a grip, Davies.

He took a deep breath. "Grayson? Can you hear me, buddy?" he called out, the weight on his body distorting the sound. "Daniel? Stevie?" The last name drew a reaction; a shallow moan, followed by a muffled groan.

"Shit, man. I think the building just whipped our ass."

A wave of hysteria rose in Tyler and he wanted to laugh so hard it vibrated along his chest. "Are you stuck?" he called out. "Can you see the others?"

"I can't see shit."

"Grayson? Daniel?" Tyler called again, worry for his team loosening some of the cobwebs in his brain.

He tried moving his feet and was relieved to discover his legs weren't pinned. That left his upper body, including his left arm. "How are you doing, Stevie?" he called when he heard the sound of loose stone hitting the floor.

"Just peachy," came the sardonic response from directly above him. A few minutes later he was free, and Stevie was offering his hand.

He took it and pulled himself upright, ignoring the tightness in his chest, to check their surroundings. He spotted Grayson pinned beneath a beam, less than a metre away, making his blood run cold. "Shit, we have to -"

A deafening, high pitched tone reverberated inside his head and he covered his ears instinctively. The ground in front of him dropped away and instead of lying among the rubble, Grayson was in a coffin surrounded by earth.

"NO!" Tyler screamed as the wood burst into flame and his friend was swallowed whole.

When his heart rate levelled, Tyler realised he was in the cottage. It had all been a dream. He was bolt-upright at the edge of the sofa; his breathing laboured, sweat coating his skin.

"Tyler?" Lilly-May's sleepy voice penetrated his shock.

He turned, taking in her heavy-lidded eyes which meant she had fallen asleep too. She was beside him before he could respond, wrapping her small arms around him.

"Shh," she whispered, though he made no sound. "You're safe. It was just a dream."

God, but he loved this woman. She was so strong, so solid, that he wanted her to continue holding him this way, just so he could know a moment's peace. But he wouldn't taint her with the darkness in him, and he didn't deserve to seek comfort when his family needed him.

"I have to go," he said, moving back so her arms slipped away. "I shouldn't be here."

She tilted her head to the side, watching him in her careful way. "Do you remember the day we met?" she asked, surprising him.

"I remember."

She held out a hand and he had to swallow past the sudden lump in his throat. "It's my turn to take care of you now. Tell me where you want to go."

He looked down at her slim, delicate hand and then covered it with his own. His fingers dwarfed hers and yet the way it felt, this gesture of friendship - it was bigger than anything he'd ever felt. "I need to be at the hospital... I left, and I -"

"Sometimes we just need a little time to figure out what's right," she whispered.

He stood and she followed, hanging onto him when he would have pulled his hand away. When Lilly-May set her mind to something she was as ferocious as a forest fire and as difficult to stop. He didn't have it in him to refuse her, so he simply walked towards the door with their fingers intertwined.

It was only when he reached her Mini that he paused. "Perhaps we should walk," he said, eying it warily. "I could fit that thing in my pocket."

She laughed, a light happy sound, and he decided he'd squeeze himself into a tin can if it meant hearing it again. It was actually roomier than it looked. He still felt like an idiot, scrunched up in the passenger seat, but at least his knees weren't behind his ears.

"Tell me something about your friend," Lilly-May said as she pulled out of the drive.

It took him a moment to respond because the heaviness had settled again, squeezing hard. "Grayson was touched by fire from a young age," he said, wondering, out of all the things he could have said, why he'd led with that. "When he was five, he got trapped in a barn when it set on fire. Gray was lucky to get out without a scratch."

He turned to her briefly, when he heard the breath catch in her throat.

"When he talked about it," he continued. "His voice was almost reverent. He had been transfixed by the dragon tearing down the building, that's how he described it. He crept under an old tractor and watched her devour the place, completely mesmerised by her beauty."

Now she turned to him, a quick glance, but he could see the question in her face.

He shrugged. "It was something we had in common, a connection to the fire. It's hard to explain, but I think fire takes on a personality because of the way it moves, how it thinks - there's a respect, a need to understand and contain." He smiled, thinking of Grayson's description. "He often said he felt no fear, back then, that the fire went about her business and didn't threaten him, wouldn't hurt him until he got in her way."

"I don't understand. Fire is destructive. It's why you put on your uniform - to save people."

He nodded. "That's definitely the main reason we serve, but for Grayson and me it's also about education, and in some way it's almost a courtship; ensuring she doesn't rage out of control, while understanding her desire to live."

"I've never heard you talk that way before." Her gaze swung towards him again. "Doesn't it scare you?"

He almost smiled. She wanted to understand and that meant something to him. "It terrifies me. I know what she's capable of, and I've seen what happens when you forget." She was silent for over a minute and he knew she was processing what he'd said.

"When did it happen for you, this...fascination with fire?"

He shifted uncomfortably, and it was nothing to do with the lack of space.

"Oh," she said, eyes on the road. "I never..."

The silence was full of tension. Tyler knew she was thinking of her parents and the fact she'd lost them both to fire. It was one of the reasons he had stopped talking to her about his job. But mostly it was because he tied his own tongue in knots.

"Grayson was the funny guy," he said. "The one who got us through a hard day at work. He had this special ability to walk the line between irritating and highly entertaining."

He saw her smile before she spoke. "I've only met him once, but it was memorable."

"How so?"

"It was the night of the Music 101 charity auction last year. I was helping out at the restaurant and everyone was a little tense, maybe even intimidated by all the celebrities in the room."

Tyler hadn't attended, but his best friend James Colby, bad boy of television, had strong armed a list of his co-workers into taking part. His brothers had closed The Winchesters to the public and hosted a special meal for the winning dates.

Lilly-May turned briefly. "Grayson had the entire room buzzing with his playful banter and jokes about putting out all the fires in the room. It was pretty great."

It hurt to think about the hole his friend had left behind. He had always been there, could make Tyler laugh with a goofy expression and knew exactly what to say when they had a bad shift. "I'm going to miss him so much."

Lilly-May took her left hand from the wheel and placed it in his. "I know."

They fell into silence again until they reached the hospital.

"Remember what I said, Ty," she murmured softly. "You're not in this alone. Anything you need, all you have to do is ask."

"Thank you." He squeezed her hand and let it go. "For everything."

It was easier than he thought to get out of the car and walk towards the hospital. All he'd needed was a little time to control the raging emotions. Now the pain was a dull ache he could handle, so it was time to step up and be there for Daniel.

He spotted Lorna Barnes as soon as he arrived on the ward. Her hair was like a beacon, especially to him, the pale gold always reminded him of another. Her eyes didn't bewitch though, and instead of green, they were a light caramel brown.

She ran forward with a loud, piercing wail and threw herself into his arms. Tyler managed to catch her, and disengage himself before she could cling.

"Ty-ty, I've been so worried about you," she breathed.

He tried not to cringe at the name, but he really wasn't up to dealing with her special brand of dramatics. "What are you doing here, Lorna?" he asked, avoiding eye contact. He was too busy trying to scope out the ward.

"Where else would I be when my guys are in trouble?"

An image of Grayson flashed into Tyler's head, making him soften. His friend had liked Lorna, and she had every right to be here. "How's Daniel?" he asked, finally looking at her. She would no doubt have as much information as the ward sisters; she was adept at worming her way in. Guilt pierced through him at the thought. He was being mean.

"We're still waiting for him to wake up. The doc isn't sure how much damage was done to his brain. There was a lot of swelling, but it's going down."

"That's good," he mumbled, feeling like shit because he should have known that. He should have been there.

"Katie finally went home to grab a change of clothes, but I expect she'll be back soon. Her father practically dragged her out of here." Her small smile turned wistful. "I know what that's like."

Lorna had been at Greg Danson's bedside, a friend they'd lost to a vehicle explosion almost two years ago. They had been on four dates before he died, but Lorna had stepped into the role of grieving widow and milked it for all it was worth.

Nice, Ty. That's real nice.

"I'll catch up with you later," he said, moving past her before he could verbalize the thoughts in his head.

He knew he was being unreasonable because of what had happened between them. In a moment of weakness he'd accepted her comfort and it had been a mistake. She had been hanging around the station for years, somehow wangled an invitation to all the events, and she saw Tyler as the ticket to securing her family.

The truth was, she made him feel weak, pathetic, and it wasn't her fault. He had been with her because she reminded him of Lilly-May. He had lost himself in the illusion, and used her because he was lonely.

Yeah, you're a real prince.

"I won't be far," she called after him, making him feel worse.

He forced himself to turn, to smile at her. "Thanks, Lorna. We all appreciate your support." Turning away again, so she didn't read too much into it, he strode down the hall towards Daniel's room.

This time he didn't leave the hospital until he was ordered to. It wouldn't have been the first time he'd ignored a command, but as it came from Daniel he figured it was for the best. The man had the constitution of an ox and nothing could bring him down - not physically anyway. He had awoken with a joke on his lips and all the bravado he'd been born with, until they'd told him about Grayson.

His face had turned deathly white, which struck Tyler as odd considering all the blood he'd lost. The roof hadn't taken him down, but the death of a brother had.

For an hour they'd sat in silence, every member of the team who wasn't on shift, mourning the loss in the quiet hospital room. Lorna was there too, and Katie, Daniel's wife, and the memories bound them all.

Finally, Daniel had ordered everyone but Katie home, at least for the evening. The fact he did it without a jibe or the crack of a smile hit Tyler where it hurt.

Now, forty minutes after returning home, he was feeling the dark curtain of grief gather around him again. The hard, sharp knock at his door reminded him he couldn't hide for long, and as he rose to answer it, he wondered which of his brothers it was.

He hadn't expected Jamie, and the sight of his best friend made him want to cry like a little girl. James Colby was a household name. He was the bad boy of day-time television and he fit the role perfectly. Especially now, with the hint of steel in his green eyes. The trademark brown hair was sporting deep grooves, like he'd been working his aggression through the thick locks. Tyler opened his mouth to speak, but was struck dumb when his friend stepped forward and hugged him hard.

"I'm sorry, man," James said, stepping back. "It's hell on earth to lose a brother."

He would know. He had lost his own brother to a fire, a fact which had cemented their friendship. They also had a sister in common - Adrienne Baxter, his brother's wife, was James' sister in all ways except blood, as she was Tyler's, long before she married Sebastian.

"Thanks, J-man."

James nodded once, stepping past him into the room. Tyler noticed the bag he carried. He watched as Jamie brought out a six-pack and pulled one free.

"What do you say we get shit faced?" James asked.

"I'd say there was a reason I like you so much."

James grinned and threw him a bottle. "Okay, Dragon-slayer, why don't you park your butt before you fall on it?"

He did feel tired, so it wouldn't take much alcohol to get him on his back. "It's really good to see you, Jamie," he said, dropping onto the couch. "I didn't think you got back till next week." His eyes narrowed. "I hope you didn't come home early on my account."

James took a long swig of beer, not to keep him waiting, but to let him know the question didn't warrant an answer. Family came first in James' book, and he was fiercely protective of his. "As I am here, we should make plans for the party tomorrow night."

"Shit, I'd forgotten about that." Dylan and Lilly-May were celebrating their thirtieth in style.

"Then you're lucky I'm here."

Tyler tilted his bottle towards him. "I'm not sure I'll make a very good date, but I'm game if you are."

"As long as our ties don't clash we're good to go."

Tyler almost choked on a mouthful of beer. "You know, I really don't need a babysitter. But I'm still glad you're here, my man."

"You said that already," James said, rolling his eyes. "Now, let's get this party started." He stretched out on the couch. "If we time it right, we'll still be drunk for the party."

"You're a cheap ass date, you know that?"

James grinned. "Yeah, but I look good."

"I'll toast to that."

Chapter 4

As it turned out, Tyler was stone cold sober when he arrived at his parents' house for the joint birthday celebration. Despite his best intentions, he hadn't drunk enough with James to warrant a hangover, though he had the bad mood down pat. He was wishing for oblivion after ten minutes surrounded by a roomful of Dylan's friends, and feeling like a horse's ass for being a mood killer.

It was obvious his mother had worked hard. The marble entrance hall was gleaming, and waiters in tuxedos were ready to greet guests with a glass of champagne as staff took their coats. The games room had been transformed into a dance hall, with tables artfully placed and colour exploding from every corner. As he wandered the lower floor, he could see evidence of all the planning. One of the sitting rooms now had a bar and a full complement of staff. The dining room had been transformed and the smell wafting through from the kitchen meant Chris was working his magic.

All Tyler wanted to do was huddle on a bar stool and get wasted, though he avoided that because of the wall length mirror. He didn't want to look at himself. Not that he hadn't made an effort. He'd squeezed into a tux, one he always kept for such an occasion. The damn thing was suffocating him, but that was nothing new. He kept moving, doing his duty and mingling.

He crossed the marble hallway, looking for a quiet spot to pull himself together, when Lilly-May arrived. The sight of her robbed every thought from his head. Her hair was pinned at the side and cascaded over her shoulder in pale blonde waves. It appeared as soft as the bronze coloured gown she wore, so silky he wanted to touch it.

"You do realise you're dribbling all over your mother's precious marble," James said, stepping up beside him.

Dragging his gaze away, he groaned. "Could I be any more pathetic?"

James' brow shot up in surprise. "Not pathetic, but you're definitely smitten."

Evidently something could lift his mood - namely James Colby using the word smitten. "Well, aren't you the cutest thing," he drawled, adding a flutter of his lashes.

"Don't be childish. It's the only way to describe those puppy dogs when they latch onto Lilly." They turned when they heard the squeal of laughter. "You really need to stop hiding in the shadows, my friend. How she hasn't figured it out yet is beyond me. It makes me want to bang your heads together."

"Am I really so transparent?" Tyler asked, watching Lilly-May and his brother, Dylan.

"It's a school boy crush that's lasted a decade. What do you think?"

Now his head snapped back around, surprised by the irritation in James' tone. "What the hell crawled up your ass?"

His friend flinched and hung his head a little as though caught doing something he shouldn't. Tyler's anger disappeared because it was James who looked like the school boy. It was a shock to realise his friend looked like hell.

"Jamie talk to me," he said, focusing his attention on the changes in James' face. Why hadn't he noticed how drawn he looked last night?

"Not here, bud. Not now. I'll be okay. You know I like to ride you about Lilly."

"What are you two cooking up?" Dylan asked.

Tyler actually jumped he was so close. He turned, meeting his brother's eyes. "We leave the cooking to other, more qualified members of the family. Great to see you, bro."

Dylan looked from one to the other with a frown, but let it drop. "We have this lovely lady to thank for talking me into this," he said, slipping an arm around Lilly-May's waist.

Tyler steeled himself to look at her, but all he could hear were James' words in his head. As though he sensed it, James slapped him on the back.

"How are you, Ty?" Lilly-May asked, with genuine concern.

Looking into her eyes, he was pleased he didn't have to force the smile. "I'm okay, thanks. Happy we're all here to help you celebrate." His gaze returned to Dylan. "Both of you."

"Thanks, bro."

James stepped forward to take Lilly-May's hand. "Happy Birthday, Lilly. You look beautiful." He waggled his brows at Dylan. "Same to you, Michelangelo."

Lilly-May's laughter floated over Tyler like a caress and he didn't catch his brother's reply. James had nicknames for them all, and since Dylan was an architect it wasn't hard to figure why. He often called Lilly-May Edesia, the Roman Goddess of food.

It wasn't until he felt their eyes on him that he realised they were waiting for some kind of response. "I'm sorry, what?"

"How's Daniel?" Lilly-May asked, frowning.

"He's going to be okay." His eyes drifted over her shoulder as his mother appeared. "Excuse me a minute," he said, stepping around them. "I'll catch up with you later."

He left them staring after him, their concern burning into his back. It was coming at him from all sides, and it made him feel like shit to see the hurt in his mother's eyes. He hadn't seen her since he'd appeared in her kitchen after the fire and holed himself up in the guest house.

Pulling her into his arms, he breathed in the familiar scent of home. "Hi, mum."

She teared up a little when he let her go. "You look so handsome," she said, straightening his tie, though it didn't need it.

"And you are the prettiest in the room." He bent to kiss her cheek. "I'm sorry I didn't call."

She shook her head and a tear rolled free. "Of all my boys you're the bravest. But it doesn't stop me from worrying."

He brushed the tear away with his thumb, the way she had done when he was small. "I know, and I promise you I'm okay. I'll always come home."

Her smile brightened her face and he felt the strength of it, as always. "Well, okay then. That's all I need to know." She linked her arm through his. "But there's someone else who needs to see you."

Tyler spotted Adrienne as soon as they entered the dining room. She looked radiant, and very beautiful in the form-fitting red dress. Dylan called her the Amazon Queen and right now she certainly looked the part with her long blonde hair pulled away from her face and plaited down her back in a thick braid.

She spotted him and rushed over, stopping a few feet away, eyes narrowed in assessment, head turned at an angle.

He laughed as he stepped forward to pick her up, and then he was swinging her in a circle, not giving a damn who was watching.

"I wasn't sure if you'd come," she whispered, squeezing him tight.

"The world keeps on turning, right, Addy?"

"As long as you're okay it does. Are you okay?"

"I'm good." He realised he was still holding her off the floor, and knew people were probably staring.

Right on cue he felt a tap on his right shoulder. "You can put my wife down now," Sebastian said, making him laugh.

He did, lowering her to the floor to face his brother, or rather his brothers, since Chris was shoulder to shoulder with him.

"Are the Winchesters going to take me outside now?" Tyler asked, grinning.

"Now, boys," their mother warned. "Don't make me march you all out there."

Adrienne chuckled softly. "You should listen to your mother."

"Indeed," Sebastian said, giving Tyler a knowing expression. "Humour us, bro."

He didn't really have a choice when Chris and Sebastian parted in a fluid move to flank him.

As they walked towards the terrace, Tyler found himself grinning again. He'd walked right into this one. "You know, boys, there's a room full of witnesses."

Chris snorted and stepped ahead to push through the double doors. "You don't get to run this time, kid."

The cool night air was a welcome break from the suffocating heat of so many bodies. He scanned the veranda and spotted his father leaning casually against the rail. "Ah oh," Tyler said, making a bee-line for him. "This smells like an intervention."

"Do you need one?" Chris asked, with a hint of amusement.

"No, but then we seem to be missing a few members of the boys club."

"Nah, we're all here."

He turned at the sound of Dylan's voice and was unsurprised to see James bringing up the rear. They had adopted him into the family and never left him out. Throwing his hands in the air, he walked to perch next to his dad.

"I lost a friend in the line of duty. I'm allowed a little down time," he grumbled.

"No doubt about that, son," his dad said, squeezing his shoulder. "And you take as much time as you need."

"Why do I get the feeling there's a but in there?"

Chris pinned him with a look. "Because, brother mine, you seem to be under the impression that you're in this alone and we're here to remind you that you're not."

He stared at them, genuinely baffled, and then realised they were right. He had a habit of internalising his pain, and Grayson's death wasn't the main cause for their concern. He'd been pulling away for months, separating himself from the family unit because he didn't want to taint it with his troubles.

"What's going on with you, Ty?" Sebastian asked, in a voice that made others shake in their boots.

"Nothing. I'm okay. I know I haven't been around as much lately, but I'm okay."

In truth he avoided most of the family gatherings because of Lilly-May. It was getting harder to hide his feelings from them, as James had already pointed out. By seeking solace in Lorna's arms he'd only made it worse, because it felt like a betrayal. It made no sense.

"If I promise to try harder can we drop this and get back to the party?"

The door opened and Connie, their sister, poked her head out. "What's this? An intervention?" she asked, wandering over.

Tyler got a lump in his throat just looking at her. She was growing up so fast, and he hadn't seen her in weeks. It wasn't unusual when she was away at university. But now she was home he could no longer hide behind the excuse. He took her in as she stopped in front of their father. Her light brown hair was short and stylish, and the dress she was wearing - a patterned print which stopped just above the knee, he knew she'd designed herself. She'd placed a matching band around her forehead, which drew attention to the blue of her eyes. They were just like his own.

"Mum's looking for you," she told their father. "It's time to make the speeches." All the men groaned, and she rolled her eyes. "I think the boys club needs to man up. Stop hiding out here and help me inject some life into this place. It's like a wake in there." Her eyes widened when she realised what she'd said. "Sorry, I didn't -"

"We're used to those size eights of yours," Chris said, stepping forward. "So while you take that classy shoe out of your mouth, why don't you come with me?" He put an arm around her shoulders. "I have a few ideas up my sleeve."

"I'll catch up with you later, Con," Tyler called after them, nodding at his father as he got up to follow.

"Do you know when it is yet? The funeral?" Sebastian asked when they left.

He shook his head. "Not yet, but I'll let you know."

"Good. We all want to be there," Dylan told him, nodding at Sebastian. "It's important."

He didn't know what to say to that, which was okay, because they didn't expect a response. When they followed the others, he stayed where he was for a moment, watching James. His friend hadn't said anything. He was looking through the glass doors to where Adrienne stood beside her sister, Lucy.

"It's about her, isn't it? Lucy, I mean."

James turned to him, his expression cloaked. "Still not the time, Ty."

"Did you ever wonder why we get on so well?" he responded quietly. "We both feel the need to deal with everything alone." He glanced into the other room. "Talk to me."

James was silent for so long he began to wonder if he would ever answer. "She thinks she might have cancer." Whatever he'd been expecting, it wasn't that. "Does Addy know?" he asked, watching their sister.

"No. I gave Lucy two days to tell her, or I will."

It wasn't a surprise. James had been protecting Adrienne most of his life. It was a hard habit to break. "How did she take that?"

"Called me a few interesting names, but she promised to do the right thing and that's all I care about."

It was clear James was lying to himself. He'd grown close to Lucy too, and didn't like to see any of his family hurting. "What can I do?" Tyler asked, when James met his eyes.

"Be there. I'm on location for a few months so I need to know you're looking out for them."

"Always." He wanted to ask why he was going away again so soon. But he didn't. The day time show he'd worked on for years was taking a seasonal break and it was usually a time when James would catch up on everything he'd missed due to his busy schedule. It seemed he wasn't the only one hiding. "Do you want to give the alcohol another try?"

"Not particularly. Perhaps we should both loosen up a little and go help Connie liven things up."

Tyler inclined his head. "You do have a reputation to keep."

"Exactly." James patted him on the back. "Let's show them how it's done."

In the end they didn't have to lift a finger. Given the guest list and the number of people the Davies' knew, they had a stream of people fighting over the microphone.

The music was enough to lift everyone's spirits, and with the champagne flowing and Chris's kitchen never closing, it was the perfect night to celebrate Dylan and Lilly-May's milestone.

It was going well until he found himself on the dance floor with Lilly-May's small form pressed against his. He'd held out as long as he could, but it was hard to refuse Lilly-May, especially since she was drunk as he'd set out to become.

They were dancing to *Ed Sheeran's Thinking Out Loud*, which was as ironic as it was excruciating. He liked the song, liked the feel of Lilly-May in his arms even more. He just wished she knew how true the lyrics were in his heart.

"I'm so glad Dylan talked me into this party," Lilly-May said, smiling up at him. She looked happy, and not because of the alcohol.

"Me too." He swallowed hard when her hands settled against his chest. "You look so beautiful tonight, Lilly."

Her smile turned dreamy. "Do you think so?"

"I… I can't do this."

"What?" she asked, frowning when he stopped moving with the music.

"Nothing. I'm just not much of a dancer." He forced a smile and resumed the gentle sway. "I'm happy you're having a good time."

She sighed and rested her head against his heart, and wouldn't you know, it was in time to Ed's words. He could smell the fruity aroma of her shampoo, mixing with the feminine scent he knew would cling to him long after the song was over. He was losing his mind, and if he didn't get a hold of himself he was going to do something really stupid.

Across the room his gaze met Dylan's, and the look of acknowledgment in his brother's eyes was like a wakeup call. As the last bars of the song played out he had to force himself not to flee the dance floor.

"Thanks for the dance," he said when she looked up at him. "I should let my brother cut in."

She glanced over her shoulder to where Dylan was leading Adrienne towards them. "I think he's got his hands full," she murmured and then giggled. "It looks like you're stuck with me."

Tyler stepped back so quickly she wobbled on her feet and he had to reach out to catch her before she fell. "I've got you," he murmured, cursing himself for his cowardice.

Lilly-May put her hand to her forehead. "Whoa, I'm pretty sure the room is not supposed to be spinning."

"Why don't you take a break for a while?" he suggested, taking her elbow.

"I think that's a good idea," she said, laughing again. "I've had more to drink than I thought."

He steered her to the tables set up beside the dance floor.

"You know what, I'd better call it a night," she said, leaning into him a little. "Would you mind letting the others know."

"Of course not." He glanced around, hoping to find Connie. Lilly-May was staying in the cottage and the way she was using his arm as a crutch, she was going to need a hand.

"I just need a minute to get my bearings and then I'll tackle those stairs."

"Stairs?"

"Yes, we had to change the sleeping arrangements. I'm upstairs in your old room because they needed the space."

The thought of her sleeping in his bed made him want to groan. How many fantasies had he had about her in that very room? The universe was surely playing a joke on him. "Let me find-"

"No." Lilly-May stood up straight, trying her hardest to appear sober. "I'm perfectly capable of finding my own way."

He thought about the staircase, the steep steps and the marble floor at the bottom.

Don't do it, Tyler. She'll be fine.

"Why don't I accompany you?" he found himself saying.

"That's silly. I'm more than capable of getting there on my own."

She's right. Let her go.

"I'm sure you are. But humour me, okay?"

Her hand found his arm again. "You're such a gentleman. Always looking out for people," she whispered, staring at him with more respect than he deserved.

He practically squirmed. He was trying so hard to fight back the image of her naked in his bed. None of his thoughts belonged to a gentleman.

Her hand slipped down to clasp his hand and he completely forget what he'd been about to say. He realised after several seconds of silence that she was still looking at him expectantly, and only then did he move.

Lilly-May was actually steadier on her feet than he'd given her credit for. She didn't lean on him again, though he began to wish she would. Strolling through the house hand in hand was beginning to feel like part of a fantasy. One where they were going to their room, where they shared a bed and he could make love to her until they were both exhausted. He had to remind himself that she'd had too much to drink.

It wouldn't be taking advantage if you were together.

"Thanks, Tyler. I appreciate you looking out for me."

He blinked at the sound of her voice, shocked when he saw they were already outside his old room. "No problem," he said, letting go of her hand. "Sleep well, Lilly."

"I doubt that," she muttered. "I hate drinking this much. The moment I lie down it's going to feel like I'm on a merry go round." She opened the door, her face relaxing. "On the other hand, I finally get to see what your room looks like."

He froze in place, unsure if he'd heard right.

"Your face," Lilly said, giggling. "Relax, Ty. I didn't mean to offend you."

"Offend me?"

"You looked so horrified for a moment, like I wanted to sneak into your room and do wicked things."

He frowned, completely losing the thread. Had she known about his fantasies? No. It wasn't possible.

"We were friends, and yet you never let me come in here," she said, bringing his thoughts back. "I used to wonder what you were hiding."

"Why would you think that?" He couldn't help the defensive note in his voice. He knew that it was the alcohol talking. That she was taking her own trip down memory lane and they were on a completely different page. None of it seemed to matter.

"Tyler?" her brows scrunched together, like she was trying to figure out what she was missing.

Leave. Right now. Walk away.

He couldn't do it. It was like drowning, he thought. She was filling his heart, his mind, his lungs - she was everywhere. "God help me," he said, and covered her surprised mouth with his. The moment their lips met he knew it was a mistake, and he would have stepped back if she hadn't wound her arms around his neck. Her fingers combed through his hair, making him groan when she made a fist and pulled him closer. How could he have known it would be like this? That she would respond so ardently. She was as seductive as any fire, and he was in danger of being burned by this one moment of weakness. It was too late now. He wanted her with a desperation he'd never known and since she was as consumed by the desire as he, he took his fill.

The sound of laughter on the stairs pierced his brain and he snapped his head back, taking Lilly-May with him. He untangled himself and set her carefully on her feet, horrified. He could barely even look at her.

"Lilly…I'm sorry…" His words trailed off at her wild-eyed stare. He'd startled her, taken advantage of her, and probably ruined whatever friendship they had. "Please forgive me." He turned, oblivious to the curious stares of the couple at the end of the corridor.

"Tyler," Lilly-May said, putting a hand on his arm. "We have to talk about this."

Steeling himself he glanced at her. "You're right. But not now. I can't do this right now." He couldn't face the questions, or the rejection.

"Okay." She dropped her hand. "We've both had something to drink, so it's probably better -"

"I've barely touched a drop," he said, knowing that would change as soon as he got home. "Which makes me the furthest thing from a gentleman doesn't it?"

She frowned, her gaze flickering over his shoulder when it registered they had company. "I don't understand."

"I know, and I'm sorry about that too." He let out a long sigh. "Get some sleep, Lilly. I'll talk to you tomorrow."

This time she let him go, and he didn't look back.

Chapter 5

Lilly-May stepped into Tyler's childhood room and closed the door. Her hand shook as she felt for the light switch, but it wasn't from the champagne she'd consumed, it was the emotions churning through her system. Tyler had kissed her, and not in an experimental meeting of lips. He'd wanted her, she'd seen the passion burning in his eyes a split second before he'd taken her mouth.

She touched her lips and sagged back against the door. She still felt him, like a piece of him had been left behind. Who knew that gentle, caring nature of his held a possessive streak that eclipsed all but the feel of him. And it had been a possession. Her body had responded on instinct, lost to the pleasure awakened at his touch. It scared her a little. She had never been kissed so thoroughly, never before wanted to give herself so freely.

"Shit," she muttered, stumbling towards the bed. What the hell had happened? Sinking into the soft mattress she thought about their brief conversation in the hall. It only confused her more.

He'd been difficult to read all evening, keeping his usual distance at social events. But when he'd danced with her, held her gently in his arms, something had changed. She hadn't tried to analyse it at the time. Now she couldn't help wondering if he'd been battling against the desire she'd read in his expression.

Forcing herself to focus on something other than the faint buzz along her skin that was a reminder of him, she glanced around the room. Veronica had clearly made changes over the years. It didn't look like a teenager's safe haven, if it ever had. It looked like a place her youngest son could lay his head whenever he came home.

A desk took up most of the facing wall and though it was clear now, save from a heavy claw lamp, it wasn't hard to imagine his books spread across the neat surface. Her gaze drifted to the bookshelf on the small wall which led to an en-suite. It held Tyler's football trophies and a collection of other sports memorabilia. He'd always enjoyed to compete. There was a wardrobe and dressing table, which she expected now stood empty, and an ottoman at the foot of the bed. None of it told her anything, and that made her wonder what she'd been expecting.

With a heavy sigh she crossed to the separate bathroom. She stripped out of her dress and hung it on a hook she found on the wall beside the door, then rolled her underwear into a ball and placed it on the sink. There was a wash basket in the corner, but she would take care of her own dirty laundry.

Smiling at the obsessive need to take care of herself, she switched on the water and stepped into the shower cubicle. The jet was cold for a moment or two, and she welcomed the cold slap against her skin. It cleared her head a little.

That was until her thoughts turned to Tyler, and the times he had stood exactly where she was. Her body flushed, making her long for the cold water again. She should not be having such thoughts about her childhood friend. More to the point, he was the first man she'd brought into a shower with her, figuratively or otherwise. She enjoyed sex, and considered herself a sensual woman. But she didn't allow anyone to take over her thoughts. In a way Tyler had always done that, something she accepted because it had never been sexual. Until now.

She washed quickly, tired of her mind's wanderings, and somehow managed to convince herself things would be clearer in the morning. Perhaps the kiss had been a by-product of the alcohol, and they would be able to laugh about it.

"I've barely touched a drop," Tyler's voice pointed out in her head, making her flush all over again.

As she climbed naked beneath the sheets of his bed she cursed herself for not retrieving her overnight bag. The friction from the soft fabric made her long for a harder, stronger weight on her body, which made her curse herself for the carnal images she was having of her friend.

"Stop it," she said aloud. "Just stop it."

The words were useless and as sleep claimed her, all she could see was Tyler's familiar face. She'd been worried about the room spinning because she'd partied too hard. She had not anticipated the effects of a kiss, and what it could do to her equilibrium.

***

Lilly-May awoke to sunlight streaming in through the bedroom window. Her head felt fuzzy, though it had nothing to do with a hangover. Everything had changed and her mind was no closer to a solution. All she wanted to do was hide under the covers so she didn't have to face her new reality.

It might have worked, if it hadn't been for the knock. She couldn't hide from that. Feeling trapped, her eyes drifted to the door and then dropped to the bed covers.

"Lilly, it's V," came a soft voice from the other side.

"Come in," she called, breathing out a sigh of relief.

Veronica slipped inside, carrying Lilly-May's overnight bag and a glass of juice. "How did you sleep, honey?"

Damn those flushes, Lilly-May thought as her face heated. She could hardly tell Tyler's mother about her eventful dreams. "Well, thank you."

Veronica didn't seem to notice her discomfort. She dropped the bag onto the ottoman and walked round with the juice. "Tyler wouldn't let me get rid of the bed," she said, arm outstretched. "It's only because it was relatively new and we have it cleaned that I agreed to keep it."

Lilly-May had no idea what to say to that so she took the orange with a smile.

"Chris is making breakfast, so you come down when you're ready."

Her eyes shot up in surprise. "He's still in the kitchen? What did he do, sleep in the sink?"

Veronica laughed. "He enjoys taking care of us, and he knows I don't get a break very often."

It was true. In fact, Chris was the only person Veronica gave free rein in her kitchen. "Then I'd better get dressed and take advantage of his hospitality."

"You do that. Dylan will be down shortly too."

She watched Veronica cross to the door. "How about Ty? Will he be joining us?"

"Unfortunately not. It's his first shift back at work today. I'm trying not to think about it. It feels too soon." Lilly-May heard the catch in Veronica's voice, but when she turned her eyes were steady. "I'll see you downstairs."

Scrambling across the bed, Lilly-May grabbed her bag and pulled it towards her. She unzipped the side pocket and pulled out her phone. The urge to hear Tyler's voice was strong, but she knew he wouldn't answer if his shift had started so she pulled up a text message. It took several attempts before she was happy with the words.

To: Tyler Davies

I hope you have an uneventful shift. Call me when you're free. I'd really like to talk to you. LM x

Fifteen minutes later, after stowing away her worry and packing her things, she was dressed and ready. The smell of cinnamon greeted her at the top of the stairs and her mouth watered. Chris had baked her favourite sticky cinnamon buns and the sentiment made her eyes burn.

She found Dylan in the kitchen, working side by side with Chris, and took a moment to watch them. "What are you two cooking up?" she asked, knowing it would make Dylan smile.

He turned with a happy grin. "There's my favourite girl."

She laughed, opening her arms to offer him a hug. Chris stepped up with a spatula in his hand, so she gave him one too.

"We have to eat in the dining room this morning," Dylan told her. "Mum is about to kick us both out of here, so we're just finishing up."

"What can I do to help?"

Chris shook his head. "Not a thing. The party isn't over till you walk out the door."

"Speaking of parties," Dylan said, nudging her towards a stool. "Where did you disappear to last night?"

She couldn't prevent the blush, they were becoming something of a habit. "I overindulged a little, so I went to bed early."

"Lightweight," Dylan said, narrowing his eyes at her. "I saw you leave the dance floor with Tyler and didn't see either of you again."

"That's because you were too busy flirting with the red-head," Chris cut in from the stove. "Ty told us the score before he cut and run."

Lilly-May didn't know whether to kiss him for the interruption or cross-examine him about exactly what kind of score, though it wasn't Tyler's way to kiss and tell, as it were.

"Is there coffee in here?" she asked, avoiding Dylan's eyes. He had that look that told her he knew she was hiding something. "I think I'm suffering from my first ever hangover."

"It's already on the table. Why don't we go through?" Dylan suggested, turning to look at Chris. "You have two minutes before mum gets back."

"I need half that," Chris mumbled, waving his spatula. "See you in there."

Lilly-May wanted to drag her feet because she knew Dylan would pounce on her distraction the moment they were alone. Luckily, Simon and Connie were already seated at the grand table. It hadn't been there the night before, having been removed for the event.

"Morning," she said brightly, choosing a seat beside Connie.

"How are you, Lilly-pot?" Simon asked, making her smile.

"I'm good, thanks, Papa Davies."

His deep baritone laugh echoed around the room, making her think of Tyler. Of the three Davies boys, he was the most like his father. "It was a wonderful party. Dylan and I are lucky you agreed to open your home."

He brushed the gratitude aside with the sweep of a hand. "It's your home too, and has been since the day you came into our lives."

"Steady on, pops," Dylan said dryly. "It's meant to be tea and toast. I can live without the tears."

Lilly-May threw a crisp linen napkin at him, even though her eyes were burning because of Simon's words. "Don't be embarrassed, D. You can let it all out."

He grinned across at her, mischief burning in his eyes. She held her breath, waiting for the comeback, but he didn't say a thing. It put her nerves on edge, but then she didn't have time to think about it because others began milling into the dining room; some she knew and some she didn't.

Still, it was a typical Davies breakfast; loud and bright and full of laughter. It wasn't quite complete though. Sebastian and Addy had returned home after the party and Tyler's absence continued to haunt her. It didn't help that she had a free day. Her deputy manager was filling in at work, so she had no plans. She'd been looking forward to it, and now it felt like self-induced torture.

"Penny for them," Dylan said, making her jump. She'd been wandering the grounds before she headed out, lost in her own thoughts.

"Just thinking about what I should do with my freedom," she hedged.

"You're as bad as Chris. You're allowed to take time off now and again." He tilted his head to the side. "But that's not what's really bothering you is it?"

She began to walk again. "I've just got a lot on my mind, that's all."

There was a beat or two of silence as he fell into step beside her. "What happened between you and Ty, Lill?"

"What makes you think something happened?"

He put a hand on her arm to stop her. "Because you get fidgety every time someone mentions his name, and he left last night after saying goodbye to everyone but me."

She frowned. "What does that have to do with anything?"

"Don't do that with me, Lilly. You know why he was avoiding me. He's convinced I'm attracted to you."

"That's ridiculous." Dylan was the brother she'd always wanted, and she knew in her heart he thought of her as his sister.

"No, it's not. He's confused about his feelings for you and I imagine he finds it hard to believe I'm not attracted to you."

"I have no idea what to do with that information. I suppose I should be flattered." When he only glared at her, she closed her eyes and blew out a long breath. "He kissed me."

"Shit," he muttered under his breath, and her eyes flew open in surprise.

"Why didn't I see it, D? If he's attracted to me. Why didn't I see it?"

He shook his head, and the sadness in his eyes worried her. "I don't know. Perhaps you were in denial too."

"Oh, so this is my fault," she said, pacing in front of him. "How long, Dylan. How long have you known he wanted more than friendship?"

"Long enough. But that's not the point. What are we going to do about it?"

"We?" She laughed, though there was no humour in it. "*We* aren't going to do anything about it."

"Lilly -"

"Don't Lilly me. You knew Tyler was attracted to me and never said a word." She stopped before him, feeling lost and completely out of her element. "I don't know what to do, D. I don't want anything to change. You're my family. All of you, and I can't ruin that."

He took her hand, his face softening. "We'll always be your family, but the kiss has already changed things and you know it."

"Shit."

His mouth turned up a little. "Just go easy on him, okay."

"I'm not angry with him. I'm confused. But, whatever happens -"

"Whoa." He held a hand up. "Back up a minute. Are you saying your feelings have changed too?"

"I think the fact they are swirling around in here," she indicated her chest, "like a volcano about to erupt, would indicate a pretty big change, so yes." She began pacing again, her mind spinning with all the thoughts vying for attention. "Put it this way. If I went with my instincts from the kiss alone, it damn near blew my head off!"

It should have been funny, the way his mouth dropped open and then closed again, and it would have been, if not for the look of pride which quickly followed it. "Who knew my little brother had the moves."

She punched him on the arm, not holding back. "Not funny."

"I'm deflecting," he said, rubbing his arm. "This scares the hell out of me. I don't want either of you hurt."

"Shit." She didn't have anything else, she really didn't, and she was talking to the wrong brother. Only Tyler could answer her questions, and they both knew that. "Look, I've got to go," she said, stopping long enough to glance at him. "I'll call you later."

"I'm here for you, Lilly. Always, okay?"

"Okay." With a final nod she hurried towards her car. She had nowhere to go, but it didn't matter. Until she spoke to Tyler she wouldn't get any peace because her brain was determined to play the kiss over and over again, and her imagination took it to a whole new level. One she had no intention of sharing with Dylan.

As she got into her car, she ignored the memory of Tyler's large frame squeezed into the passenger seat and knew she needed one hell of a distraction to distance herself completely. She ended up at the sports centre, where she challenged anyone who was game to a round of squash and annihilated every single one of them. It would be remiss of her not to honour her record, and with the amount of energy coursing through her veins, it was just what she needed to shut everything else down.

Still, she waited all day for a message from Tyler, but it never came. Not even when she left him a voice mail. It was just another layer of uncertainty with which to torture herself. They had to talk about it, because it was impossible to pretend it hadn't happened, and the longer the silence stretched between them the harder it would become. She knew the best possible outcome would be to air things out and move on. It was dangerous to consider the alternative, no matter how much she wanted a repeat performance. The knowledge baffled her, yet it was undeniable. She'd felt something powerful in Tyler's arms and wanted to explore it. The only problem was, she avoided relationships because she could never see herself committing to anyone long term.

Her mother had done that, and it had stripped away the happy, vibrant woman until there was nothing left but a shell. Lilly-May felt her father's betrayal like a stain on her soul, and yet her mother had been the one he'd cheated on. She knew it was unfair to burden other men with the sins of her father, but her protective instincts stemmed from a child's heartbreak. She couldn't hurt Tyler that way. If they became lovers there was a real possibility it would destroy the precious trust they shared.

She knew all that and yet she wanted so much more than an impulsive kiss. She wanted too much.

Chapter 6

"I wish I'd seen that one coming," Stevie muttered as he passed Tyler on the way to the rig.

"Looks can be deceiving," he answered, because nobody knew that better than him. When people looked at him they saw a rich boy; they saw his father, his brother, and all their success. They didn't see him.

That changed the moment he put on his uniform, but it wasn't why he chose to wear it. Fire had claimed him early. When he'd been the arrogant kid who'd thought himself indestructible. Maybe he was, back then, but he'd recognised what her power could do and he hadn't backed away.

She could deceive anybody. Often when he arrived at a scene he saw optimism, that last glimpse of hope in the faces around him. They'd looked at the structure and judged it sound. It was holding the fire. It was strong.

But they didn't see the nature of the beast. Tyler knew the destruction she was capable of. If a building looked sound, the bitch was working that much harder to tear it down. To devour. To conquer.

Tonight had been no exception. Tyler knew how hard she fought and, god, but she was beautiful. Her flames had danced around the room, seducing all in their path.

"Grayson would have loved this," he said, though Steve was out of earshot. He had always thrived on a challenge, and there was something exhilarating about taking her on. They never took her for granted, never assumed they knew what she would do next because fire was rarely predictable. They might be able to guess where she would go, how she would react, but they never assumed to have all the answers.

It had been a solid victory, and now that the last of the flames were out, Tyler could give thanks that his team had made it out unscathed.

He bowed his head to pay his respect, as she had respected their ability to control the inferno. It was something he would have done with his friend by his side. So he took an extra moment to gather his thoughts, to separate himself from the rest.

The crowds had thinned, and only a few remained. He scanned the area and came to rest on the tree beside the house. The glow cast from the dying embers illuminated it in a deep shade of red and gold. The heat in the trunk, coupled with the blackened branches, made it appear to be bowing towards the creature who could have destroyed everything in her path. Tyler saw the beauty in it, and as he studied the fine lines and unwavering strength, he saw Lilly-May. Not that thoughts of her were ever far away. He remembered how people assumed she would bow under the pressure when her parents died and the scandal hit. That she wasn't strong enough to make it on her own.

But Tyler had known the truth. He always had. When he looked into her deep green eyes and saw the determination, he had no doubt she'd survive. Those who assumed failure weren't looking in the right direction. They were distracted by her delicate bone structure and petite form. Tyler saw those things, but didn't take them for granted.

No, he didn't take them for granted, but there was a good chance he had ruined their friendship because he'd lost himself in a moment of weakness and crossed the line. As he climbed into the rig, the exhaustion he'd been dragging around settled on him like a lead weight. He was barely conscious on the trip back to the station. The gentle hum of the engine and the buzz of voices began to blur. Normally he would be joining the conversation, but nobody pressed him on it. They were all subdued, and had been all shift. Grayson's absence was like a gaping hole none of them knew how to fill.

"You look like shit, my man," Stevie said as they pulled into the station.

"I feel like shit." He rubbed a hand over his face. "I really need some sleep before I fall on my ass."

They were silent as they began to sort through the equipment.

After a while, Stevie looked up. "Bad dreams?"

"That and I did something really stupid, like kiss Lilly-May." He hadn't meant to say it, wanted to take it back, but it was too late.

Steve whistled long and loud. "Jesus, Davies, your timing could be better. What happened?"

What happened indeed? She'd kissed him back, that's what. But she'd also been drunk and taken by surprise. "What do you think happened?" He caught sight of Stevie's expression and groaned. "Okay, scratch that. I don't even want to go there."

"Did she freak out?"

"I didn't give her the chance, I got the hell out of there like the coward I am." It still preyed on him.

"If you're a coward, my friend, it's only when it comes to her." Stevie slapped him on the shoulder. "She's your god-damn Achilles heel."

"You can be an ass, you know that, right?"

"Hey," Stevie said, raising his hands. "Don't take your frustrations out on me. I'm happy things came to a head. You've been moping around for years."

"I'm sorry my misery is so irritating." He ran a hand through his hair, wishing for an end to the conversation. "Do you fancy a round in the gym when we're finished here?"

Stevie eyed him suspiciously. "Yeah like I want you spotting me. You can barely lift your feet."

Before Stevie could predict the move, Tyler lifted him off the ground, and would have gone for the fireman's lift if he hadn't squirmed so hard.

"Okay, you've made your point," Stevie said, dropping to the floor. "You need to use that frustration on better pursuits."

"Still not going there."

"More fool you," Stevie said, and laughed. It drew the attention of the others, and for twenty minutes it was like old times.

He never got to the gym, and regretted the decision to skip out as soon as he saw who was waiting for him at home.

"How did it go?" Dylan asked, lounging on the front step.

Tyler shrugged, feeling too much emotion in his tired body. "We slayed the dragon."

His brother smiled, but it didn't reach his eyes.

"She told you," Tyler said, stepping past him to open the door.

Dylan didn't answer until they were inside. "She also told me you're avoiding her calls."

"I'm not avoiding her calls." It was a lie and they both knew it.

"Look, bro, I can see you're fighting just to stand up, so I'm going to make this easy on both of us and then get out of your hair." He paused long enough to make sure Tyler was looking at him. "There's nothing between us."

"That's not true and you know it," Tyler said, because they'd had this discussion before.

"God-damn it Ty, I'm so sick of being used as an excuse."

"An excuse?" Tyler shot back. "You think I'm using you as an excuse?"

His brother took a step forward, his face softening. "You're scared, and I get that, but it's time you both stopped leaning on me." He held a hand up when Tyler opened his mouth to speak. "Lilly uses me to distance herself from relationships, and I allow it because she's family, and because it's harmless. I didn't see what it meant to you until it was too late, and by then I knew you wouldn't listen."

Tyler considered, and heard the truth. "What makes you think I'll listen now?"

"Because you're my brother," Dylan said, clasping his shoulder. "And I won't let this come between us. If you don't want to face what happened between you at the party, that's your decision. But it won't be because of me."

The silence stretched until Tyler felt himself sag beneath the weight of it. "It's getting harder to convince myself that friendship is enough," he said on a heavy sigh. "But you were wrong about me being afraid because…I'm terrified."

Dylan chuckled before stepping back. "Some things are worth fighting for." He walked towards the door. "Now get some sleep and I'll be back to rain on your parade later."

Tyler didn't stop his brother from leaving. He should have, but it was easier on both of them. "Thanks, D."

A quick salute and he was gone, leaving Tyler to ponder.

"Sleep first," he muttered, because Dylan had been right about that too, he was fighting just to stand upright.

He had just enough juice left to shower, so padded to the bathroom to wash away the grime and dirt of the shift. It was something he usually did at the station, but he liked the idea of falling into his bed and sleeping the rest of the day away.

Stepping out of the shower, he hung a towel around his hips and crossed into the bedroom. Every muscle ached, and beneath it all was a gnawing hunger in his gut. What he wanted was to drop face down onto the bed, but he needed to replenish the energy he'd burned while fighting a fire he still felt along his skin. She had been one tough bitch, and taken everything he had. Pulling on a pair of shorts, he forced his legs towards the kitchen, where he hoped he had more than cereal. Chris had cooked up a batch of meals for him to nuke. There was a chance he had something left in the freezer.

"Terrific," he muttered, staring into the empty shelves. It appeared he would have to make do with cereal after all.

The doorbell sounded, and he frowned as he headed across. "Come to rain on my parade so soon?" he said, pulling the door open.

His brain short-circuited when he saw Lilly-May, looking as inviting as a summer's day.

"Sorry to disappoint you. But I came for answers," she said, her eyes dropping to his naked chest.

He fought the urge to fidget under her scrutiny and stepped back. "I thought you were Dylan." God, he sounded like an idiot.

"You can't avoid me forever, Ty. I've left several messages-"

"I haven't had a chance to check my phone. I was called to an emergency." He walked to the laundry basket on the coffee table, grabbed a t-shirt from the pile, and pulled it over his head. "Look, I'm sorry, okay. I planned to stop by tomorrow." He tugged his hands through his hair and turned to face her. "I…I'm sorry I crossed the line. I don't know what else to say to you."

She took a step forward, her face a mask of confusion. "That's not good enough, Ty. And I didn't come here for an apology." She tipped her head to the side, studying him. It was so familiar he almost smiled. "Where did it come from?"

I've loved you since I was four years old.

"I don't know how to answer that. It was a… moment of weakness-" He broke off at her snort of derision, tensing.

"I know you, Ty, and you're rarely impulsive. It was more than simple curiosity. I felt it."

His heart kicked against his chest. Within the frantic beat sat a desperation he couldn't define. "I don't want this to ruin our friendship." It was almost a plea. "But you're right, I can't pretend I don't want you. Not anymore."

She opened her mouth to say something, and then closed it again. Yet he waited, because he could see the questions in her eyes.

It didn't take her long. "Why didn't you tell me?"

"I was terrified of what it would do to us. I still am."

This time the silence was calmer, less intense.

"I haven't been able to stop thinking about the kiss." Her green eyes were darker, as though she were remembering it as he had.

"Me either." It was a quiet admission.

She held his gaze for the longest time, so long he wondered if she was waiting for him to say something else. But then she looked over his shoulder, her attention on the cupboard he'd failed to close. "Were you about to eat?" she asked, not waiting for a response.

"Lilly?" He turned to watch her nervous movements as she walked towards the cupboard.

"Throwing cereal into a bowl does not constitute a healthy snack." She turned to him when he said nothing. "Sorry. I thought I knew what I wanted to say, but it appears I still have a few things to work out." Her slim shoulders lifted in a shrug. "I need to keep my hands busy."

It was unusual for her to lose her composure, and he couldn't tell if that was a good thing. "Knock yourself out," he said, dropping onto a stool.

"How about gypsy toast?" She plucked a carton of eggs from the fridge, and the remainder of a loaf from the breadbin. "It keeps with the breakfast theme, plus it's all I've got to work with." His stomach rumbled, making her laugh. "I'll take that as a yes."

Before she searched out a bowl, she pulled a beer from the fridge and handed it to him. "I was going to make coffee, but I don't think my nerves can take it."

"Beer's good." He took a swig and handed it back, since she hadn't taken one for herself. The fact she almost drained the bottle made his lips twitch. "Drinking is what got us into this mess."

"You've got nothing to worry about. You were a perfect gentleman."

He swallowed hard, wondering if he'd imagined the note of disappointment in her voice. "I wasn't thinking like a gentleman."

Her gaze flew to his, the light flush on her cheeks reflecting the heat in her eyes.

He didn't know if it was the fatigue talking or a response to the way she was looking at him, but he decided to take a chance. "I imagined you in my bed, wrapped around me as I devoured every inch of your body."

"Oh god," she said in a rush of breath, dropping her head as she braced herself against the counter. It took him a second to realise she was laughing. When her head popped up he could see the merriment reflected in her eyes. "Imagine waking up in that bed after a night of erotic dreams, to be faced with you mother. I swear I didn't know where to put myself."

He felt the impact of her words like a blow, lancing his heart and stealing his common sense. "You had erotic dreams about me?"

Could you sound any more pathetic?

"That's the thing," she said when the laughter died. "These feelings, they came out of nowhere, at least for me. It's like you scrambled my brain."

Tyler found he liked the idea – very much. Still, he withheld the smile because she was back to being nervous again. It was only when she returned to her task that his grin broke free.

Her hands were sure and capable as she mixed the ingredients. No, mix wasn't the right term - she was beating the eggs into submission. When she stopped abruptly, looking at him from across the counter, his mouth actually watered.

"I don't want to hurt you," she said, with such panic in her voice he found himself moving forward.

"Why would you hurt me?"

Because she might decide to walk away.

"Because I'm the impulsive one, and, if I take a leap, I could ruin everything."

He had to force the next words through his lips. "We are friends, Lilly. If things change and it isn't what we want, we just go back to how things were."

"And you could live with that?" she asked.

"Yes."

Liar.

Her eyes searched his face, and he thought she'd seen too much. "I need to know it wasn't in my head. That I didn't dream it," she whispered, placing her hand on his chest.

He felt her heat like a brand. It burnt through his remaining fear, because he was tired of living a lie. There was no hesitation now. He gave her what she asked, what he needed, by closing his mouth over hers.

Her low, throaty moan was a spark to the inferno burning inside him. Her lips were demanding, her hands sliding possessively into his hair. He'd thought their first kiss had the ability to destroy him, but this, this was something else. The realisation he could light her up this way was dangerous.

"Shit," she said, breaking the kiss, and all the remaining tension.

He laughed, despite her frustrated curse. "Not quite the response I was looking for." Her narrow-eyed stare only made him laugh harder.

Lilly-May's expression snapped from worry to interest in a heartbeat. "How long were you thinking about it before you put this sexy mouth to work?"

That shut him up. "Long enough."

She closed her eyes, as though savouring the response. "I had so many good reasons why we shouldn't do this, and now I can't remember a single one." She stepped back, smoothing a hand down her hair. "I want more of you, Tyler, but we're going to do this right."

He could only stare at her, his mind still working on the wanting more part.

Hell yes.

"So I'm going to leave before that mouth of yours gets me into any more trouble." She turned and headed towards the door. "I'll see you tomorrow night," she said over her shoulder. "When you pick me up for our date."

Finding his voice at last, he stopped her in her tracks. "Who said anything about a date? Maybe I just want your body."

Her chuckle was low and as sexy as hell. "We'll get to that."

He almost swallowed his own tongue, which was nothing new when it came to Lilly-May.

She paused at the door, her eyes alight with an interest he'd never seen before. "Don't leave the mixture too long."

She was gone before he could think of a reply.

Chapter 7

Tyler was close to pacing a groove in his living room floor when the phone rang. He snatched up the handset, the tune grating on his nerves for no other reason than it reminded him of Grayson. Even from the grave his friend could still ride his ass. *We Didn't Start The Fire* was about as funny as a car crash right now.

"Yeah," he barked, without checking the display.

"Well, hello to you too," came Addy's throaty response. There was a damn good reason she was so popular on the radio – her voice was pure sin.

"Sorry. Bad day…" He let that hang, wondering why he'd answered the phone when he was wound so tight he was about to blow.

"I thought you had a date tonight?" she asked, trying to hide the concern and failing miserably. "Did something come up?"

He let out a long breath. "Yes and no. I'm trying to decide whether I should-"

"If you say cancel I'm going to come over there and-"

"It was started deliberately, Addy," he said, almost amused by the way they talked over each other. "Grayson died because someone purposely set the warehouse on fire."

There was a long, heavy silence, and he knew she was thinking of the past, of the fire that had stolen her family. That had been set deliberately too.

"I'm so sorry. What can I do?"

He lowered himself onto the couch, wishing he had that answer. "Talk to me, I guess. I have an hour until I'm supposed to pick Lilly up. I've waited…too long for this and I don't want-"

"She'd understand. If you told her what happened, she'd-"

"Are you ever going to let me finish a sentence?" he asked, smiling now.

"We've been playing this game too long to stop now." There was a smile in her voice too. "I was going to give you a hard time for keeping me in the dark, but-"

"James has a big mouth," he finished. "I knew he'd never be able to resist calling you, and it saved me the job."

Her snort was a reprimand in his ear. "And by save you the job, you mean you didn't want to face the questions until you were ready."

"You really think Colby let me off the hook?"

There was music now as her laughter settled around him. "You didn't mean to tell him did you?"

He thought about his friend's flying visit that morning. "No, I never mean to tell Jamie anything." The fact was, he'd spilled the beans to take James' mind of his own troubles. He'd given Addy's sister an ultimatum and asked Tyler to be there for the fall out. "How's Lucy?" he asked, with the subtlety of a brick.

"She's good, why…do you know something I don't?"

It was all he could do not to beat himself over the head with the phone. "Like I could keep anything from you."

The pause told him she didn't buy that for a second. "Tyler. What's going on?"

"You know when you asked what you could do?" he said, wishing he'd let the call go to voicemail. "You can pretend I didn't say anything."

Another silence, this one much longer. "Fine, but only because we're having lunch tomorrow and I plan to confront her. James has been acting weird since he got back and Lucy is hiding something."

It was a relief to know he hadn't completely put his foot in it. "I'm sorry I didn't tell you about the date," he said, because it was the truth. He had always relied on her to be his voice of reason. "I honestly thought I'd blown it when I kissed her-"

"What? You kissed her?"

This time he did smack the phone against his head.

She laughed. "Don't think breaking the screen on that thick skull of yours will let you off the hook. This is huge…I can't believe she didn't tell me."

"It kind of took us both by surprise," he said, groaning into the phone. "I never expected she might be-"

"Tyler Davies, I'm going to come over there and hit you with that phone myself. Why wouldn't she be attracted to you?"

He rolled his eyes. "Oh, I don't know…because we're family?"

"Lilly might be a card-carrying member of the Davies clan, but you shouldn't use that as an excuse to hide your feelings."

"Well, it seems the cat is well and truly out of the bag!" He laughed at the absurdity of it all. "I keep trying to tell myself it would be better to forget it ever happened. But she felt something too, Addy and, frankly, it scares me to death."

"Have you told her how you feel?"

The concern was back, and he knew he couldn't avoid what was coming. "I'm not sure telling her I love her is the right way to go, considering we haven't even been on a date."

"You know what I'm going to say next don't you?" There was a tenderness in her voice that made his heart ache.

"That I should be careful, because-"

"No, Ty, that's not it. You're too careful, and don't get me wrong, the last thing I want is for you to get hurt. But all I really want to say, and what I called to tell you, is that you need to be yourself." When he didn't respond she filled the silence. "You deserve to be happy, brother of my heart, and so does she."

"I don't know what-"

"To say? Don't say anything. There's nothing you can do to change the past, so go, enjoy your night, and let the investigators do their job. You can worry about that tomorrow."

"I knew there was a reason I kept you around!" It was an old joke, and he knew it would make her smile.

"Please, I haven't been able to get rid of you since the day we met." She paused for a beat or two. "Sebastian wants you to know he's going to disown you if you screw this up."

"Jesus, did James take out an ad?" He groaned when he heard the sound of his brother's laughter. "You can tell him I never liked him that much anyway." From the deep rumble down the phone line he figured she'd switched to speaker. "I'm hanging up now."

"I want details," Sebastian said, sounding way too happy about his discomfort.

"I'll be sure to pass them to Jamie."

"Touché. Night bro."

He hung up after grumbling through a goodbye, but he was smiling, and he no longer felt like walking a groove in his floor.

Forty minutes later, as he walked up the path to Lilly-May's door, the conversation with Addy replayed in his head. She'd surprised him, because he'd expected her to tell him to play it safe. But then, he'd always played it safe, so he was probably projecting.

He couldn't help wondering what Lilly-May would do if he followed Addy's advice, and as if his body rebelled at the notion, his feet froze just shy of the first step. He knew why – Lilly May was a beautiful, sensual creature, driven by curiosity, and when it burned away he would be a pile of ash.

The same fierce determination he used to confront a fire spread through his system. He could do this. Then she opened the door and he could barely breathe, let alone move.

She'd left her hair down, so it caressed the edge of her slender shoulders. The gold hue of her skin was untouched, making him want to groan. She wore a deep blue strapless dress, which clung to her generous curves and stopped just below the knee.

Sweet Jesus, I'm in trouble!

"Thank you," she breathed, her green eyes sparkling. "Though, if you keep looking at me like that, we may not make it to dinner."

Tyler grinned, he couldn't help it. He wasn't even embarrassed she'd seen his reaction, he was through with hiding. "How about we skip to dessert?"

She laughed with delight. "You've been keeping secrets from me," she said, closing the door and turning the key.

"Secrets?"

Her shoulders lifted in a careless shrug, pulling his eyes away from her face. He wanted to sink his teeth into that soft flesh.

So much trouble.

"I always knew you were charming, but I've never seen the effects first hand."

"That's because, where you're concerned, I'm usually trying not to trip over my tongue."

What the hell is wrong with me?

Her eyes widened in shock, a moment before she smiled. "Who are you, and what have you done with Tyler?"

He groaned at the reminder. She only saw him as the quietly serious and loyal member of their group. A family she'd claimed as her own. But there was no going back. Not now. "Promise me something, Lilly," he said, needing them to be clear on this one thing. "Promise me, whatever happens, this won't come between us."

She searched his face, all traces of humour gone. "I promise. Whatever happens, you'll always be my friend."

It should have discouraged him, yet he was oddly soothed by the term. His heart might be in tatters by the end of this, but he wouldn't lose her completely.

Enough with the drama, Ty.

"In that case," he said, moving up a step so they were nice and close. "Good evening, Lilly."

Before she could reply he bent his neck, and did what he'd wanted to do since the moment she stepped out of the house. Pushing aside her hair, he placed his lips against her shoulder and kissed the smooth skin.

Her sharp intake of breath had arousal beating in his blood, so he stole the sound with his mouth. She came alive, her arms locking around his neck as she tried to get closer.

It was a wild thing, the fire building between them. Every thought in his head snapped out, until there was only Lilly-May.

This time she was the one to break the kiss. Her breathing was choppy, her skin flushed. She had never looked sexier. "Perhaps we'd better go. Before we give the neighbours a show they'll never forget."

His smile was wicked, a no holds barred glimpse of exactly what he thought of the idea. "Your chariot awaits," he said, stepping aside and offering his hand.

Her eyes shot to the Porsche, before flicking back to him. "You brought out the big guns."

"She's new. I thought I'd take her for a ride." He didn't bother to hide the meaning in his statement and was rewarded when her cheeks flushed. It disarmed him, pleased him that the tables had turned and she was the one at a loss for words.

Still, she took his hand and allowed him to lead her to the car. She didn't speak until they were seated. "You Davies boys have always had fine taste in automobiles."

He grunted. "Chris wouldn't know what a fine vehicle was if it followed him home." When she only looked confused, he elaborated. "He's had his truck for ten years and I swear things are growing in there."

She laughed as she snapped her seatbelt in place. "Where are you taking me anyway? Will we be enjoying the spoils of Chris' labour?"

Tyler glanced across with mock outrage. "I may be rusty at this, but when I take a woman to dinner, I do not take her to my brothers' restaurant." Thumbing the engine, he let the purr settle around them. "You might want to hold on," he added and pulled out onto the street.

***

Lilly-May felt her stomach flutter. Not from the speed of such a powerful engine, but from the intensity of the man by her side. She didn't know this side of Tyler, she hadn't been joking about that. He was unrecognisable, and it excited her almost as much as it frightened her.

She had noticed the difference in him the moment she stepped out of the house. He had never looked at her with such naked desire. Her skin still tingled from the memory of it. It had been like a caress, the way his eyes devoured her.

It had been all she could do not to step back inside and drag him with her. Instead, she'd tried to make light of the growing tension by teasing him. His reaction had been as unexpected as their raging attraction. How had she not seen it before? This spark? The moment he touched her it lit her up inside. Her body had never betrayed her so readily, like she was attuned to his touch alone.

Get a grip, Lilly, and enjoy the ride.

Her cheeks flushed at the thought and she squirmed in her seat as erotic images filtered though her mind. He was her friend, for god's sake.

"What are you thinking about?" Tyler asked, glancing across.

"Indecent things," she said before she could stop herself, and then laughed when Tyler's foot slipped off the accelerator and hit the break. "Seriously, Ty. I don't know what the hell has gotten into me." She let out a long breath. "Is it hot in here? It feels hot." The window came down a second later and she threw him a grateful look.

"Is it too weird?" he asked, hands tensing on the steering wheel.

"That's just it. It doesn't feel strange at all. It's like the desire was always there and you woke the sleeping lion."

His swallow was audible. "I can't process that and drive. I'm having a hard enough time as it is." His husky tone shivered across her skin. She was in so much trouble. The surprising thing was, she didn't much care.

They didn't speak again until he pulled onto a quiet street on the edge of town. She narrowed her eyes and looked through the windscreen. The headlights cast a narrow beam onto the road. At either side, soft light glowed from behind windows and she thought briefly about the people on the other side.

"It's a short walk to the restaurant," Tyler said, pulling into a vacant slot.

"A walk would be nice."

He frowned at the polite tone, but all he said was, "Wait there," then hopped out and moved round to her door. She stood beside him on the street, and his face relaxed again. "Later," he told her, grinning. "I thought we could make out at the top of St Giles Hill."

"That would depend on how the date goes," she said demurely, winking. "But I'd say your chances are good."

He ducked back inside the car to grab his jacket, before settling it over her shoulders. "Game on."

The jacket was way too big for her, but she didn't mind. It wasn't unusual that Tyler wanted to take care of her. The feel of his fingers as they intertwined with hers also felt oddly familiar; a merging of the old with the new.

They walked in companionable silence along the pretty street. It was a lovely night, the perfect night for a romantic rendezvous above the city. Winchester looked beautiful at night.

She knew before they stopped which restaurant he would take her to. "Does it make you feel better that Gerard trained with Chris?" she asked, as he led her inside.

The room was bold, bright and adventurous. It suited the atmosphere as they were greeted by a colourfully dressed waitress, against a backdrop of excited chatter. Gerard Duncan had trained under Chris before setting up on his own and his huge personality was like a stamp on the restaurant.

"Chris respects him and so do I," he said, pausing to confirm the booking. The waitress came to attention immediately, the poor girl looking star-struck as Tyler glanced her way. It wasn't the first time Lilly-May had noticed his effect on women, but it was the first time it had bothered her.

Shaking off her unease, she followed Tyler as they were led to their table. It was towards the back of the room in a corner booth which afforded an air of privacy, and was the best seat in the house.

Her gaze flicked over the high-backed chair as Tyler pulled it out for her. It was covered in a deep-red fabric, which coordinated with the splashes of colour in the crisp, linen table cloth.

When they were seated, the waitress stepped forward. "I'm Stephanie, and I'll be back to take your drinks order in a few minutes."

Tyler nodded briefly in her direction. "Thank you."

He'd barely looked at her, Lilly-May thought, as their eyes met. She almost felt sorry for the girl. Almost. She couldn't pretend she didn't like being the centre of his attention. Now she thought about it, he always made her feel that way.

"Did I tell you how beautiful you look?" he asked, his voice low, intimate.

"Not in so many words, but the message was pretty clear," she said, smiling with pleasure at the memory.

He reached for her hand across the table. "I hope you don't mind, but Gerard is preparing something special for us tonight."

"How could I mind that?" she asked, though her voice wasn't quite steady.

As though sensing her nerves he gave her hand a gentle squeeze. "Relax, Lilly. It's just a pleasant meal between friends."

Her throat tightened because they were already more than that. "Do you plan to make out with all your friends?"

"Only the pretty ones."

She laughed, relaxing a little. "I'm not sure how to behave," she admitted. "These feelings are so new, so unexpected." Her smile turned playful. "I was ready to do battle when I saw the way Stephanie was looking at you."

"Now that's an interesting thought."

Her fingers squeezed his in a gentle reprimand. "I'm serious. I'm used to women drooling over you. It shouldn't be a surprise."

"She's barely out of college," he muttered, rolling his eyes.

"Oh, okay, old man!"

His grin was evil, she felt the effects of it right down to her toes.

"Can I get you something to drink?" Stephanie asked, breaking the moment. Lilly-May hadn't even seen her approach.

"I'll have a Beck's Blue," Tyler said, glancing her way.

Lilly-May waited until Stephanie's deep brown eyes met hers. "I'll have the same." She added a bright smile to ease some of her guilt. When Stephanie left them alone she leant across the table. "I want a clear head tonight."

Tyler's blue eyes glinted, and then his gaze dropped to her mouth. Her lips began to tingle at the memory of their kiss.

"Then again, maybe I need a drink after all...the anticipation is killing me!"

His eyes closed as though to savour the images in his head. "I think," he murmured, without opening them. "If we don't change the subject, your neighbours aren't the only ones who'll be getting a show."

Can we get the bill please?

"In that case. Why don't you tell me about your day? Did you put out any fires? Save any kittens from trees?" Tyler's mood changed so quickly she regretted her flippant tone. "What is it?"

"I found out today that the Rutherford Towers fire was the work of an arsonist."

Her stomach dropped, all playfulness evaporating under the force of such a blow. "I'm so sorry," she whispered, squeezing his hand.

"No, I'm sorry. I didn't mean to bring it up." He made a valiant effort to smile. "Addy told me to let the investigators handle it and she's right. There's nothing I can do about it until we know more."

Lilly-May heard the dangerous edge to his tone, the things he didn't say. She wanted to push him, if only to reassure herself he wouldn't do anything stupid, but she didn't want to fight. No, she wanted to see the light play across his eyes again.

"As long as you know I'm here for you if you want to talk about it." She sat up straighter when Stephanie returned with their drinks.

"Speaking of Addy," Tyler said, nodding his thanks for the beer. "Did you see the video of Elijah?" The tension drained from his body as soon as he spoke of his nephew.

"I'm not sure, but I saw him in person yesterday afternoon." Her lips curved at the memory. "He can say my name."

Tyler scowled. "He can't talk yet, he's only six months."

She snorted at his naivety. "He's seven months and he's a Davies. He came out of the womb charming the nurses. And he can sound out Lill, which is close enough." Her eyes sparkled with mischief. "I've been repeating the sound over and over until he mastered it."

"Sneaky," he said, grinning.

They were interrupted again when a waiter brought them the chef's special. The goat's cheese was exquisite, a well-orchestrated symphony of textures and flavours. It was followed by sea bass, close to the best she had ever tasted.

"No wonder Gerard is Chris' protégé," she mumbled, savouring the last bite.

"You can complement him personally," Tyler said, nodding over her shoulder. "He's on his way to push his advantage, now he's seduced you with food."

She laughed in delight, turning to sing his praises the moment he reached their table.

"This from a woman who is responsible for my growing waistline," Gerard answered, patting his stomach for effect, though there wasn't an inch of spare flesh on him. "I can never resist your pastries."

Lilly-May flushed at the compliment. "The next one is on the house."

Gerard slapped a hand to his heart. "You have my undying devotion."

"I'm sure Patricia will have something to say about that," Tyler drawled, speaking of the other man's wife.

"You wouldn't understand," Gerard said, shaking his head sadly. "But you have excellent taste in companions, so there's hope for you yet." He waved his arm at a passing waiter and a few moments later was handed a small picnic basket.

"As requested," he said, bowing slightly towards Tyler. "Enjoy." He turned back to Lilly-May and took her hand. "It was a pleasure," he murmured, dark eyes flashing before he brushed a kiss along her knuckles.

When they were alone, Lilly-May smiled in delight. "He learnt more than his culinary skills as Chris' apprentice."

"I'm fortunate he's happily married, otherwise I'd have a fight on my hands."

She shook her head. "There's no contest."

Tyler's smile was resplendent, transforming his already handsome features into the dangerous category.

"Shall we take our walk?" he asked, with eyes that promised it would be no casual stroll in the park.

For the first time in a long time, words failed her. All she could manage was a simple nod. He took her hand again when they were outside, and led her along the route to St Giles' Hill.

"What's in the basket?" she asked, as they made the steady climb.

"Gerard's signature dish. He made me promise a full report of your reaction." He squeezed her hand lightly. "It's a true sign of his respect, that he values your opinion about his dessert."

She rolled her eyes. "Since when did I become the authority on pastry?"

"Since half of Winchester can be found queuing at your door. Café 101 owes its success to you, in part because of the bakery you added."

"It's more to do with your brother's shrewd business sense, but I appreciate the vote of confidence."

He turned his head to look at her, and she could almost see the reprimand. "Don't sell yourself short, Lilly. Sure, Sebastian knows a good thing when he sees one, but we all respect your skills."

She thought about the joy it gave her, the pleasure of creating her menu for the shop. "Then that's icing on the cake," she said, grinning. "Because I love what I do."

They fell silent, a companionable space they didn't need to fill. Lilly-May didn't speak again until they reached the lookout point.

"I'd forgotten how magical it looks from here," she breathed. Winchester was her home, but she never grew tired of its charm; the bright lights of the city filled her with a sense of wonder.

"You're beautiful," Tyler said, his eyes on her instead of the view.

"Tyler-"

He crushed her to his chest, his hand threading through her hair so he could angle her face where he wanted it. She was spellbound by the light of desire in his eyes, and words no longer seemed important.

He dipped his head, torturing her with anticipation. It buzzed along her skin, a heat which ignited when he brushed his lips across hers.

She had never enjoyed kissing, couldn't understand why women gave so much credit to the act. Kissing Tyler was quickly becoming a lesson in the art, so instead of being impatient and letting the passion burn her up, she sank into the pleasure of it.

"Beautiful," he murmured against her mouth, making her groan when he sank his teeth into her lower lip.

"Take me home, Tyler. I want to be alone with you."

His swallow was audible, making her smile. She wasn't the only one who felt the nerves. "Believe me, I want nothing more," he said, turning her in his arms so she had her back to his chest. The hard planes of him were like torture, especially when he wrapped his arms around her. "But I want to savour this night, Lilly. I've waited so long to be with you like this."

The butterflies exploded in her stomach, thousands of tiny wings which made her want to break free from his hold on her. She didn't want his devotion, she wanted his desire.

They stood for a long time, staring into the heart of Winchester, until her pulse began to slow and she found her centre again. "I seem to remember someone promising me dessert," she said, putting her hands over his.

Releasing her, he bent to snag the basket and took her hand. "I know the perfect spot."

Tyler led her to a picnic bench, hidden beneath a copse of trees. She watched him as he unpacked the contents, enjoying the simple pleasure in studying him.

He had such focus, such strength. It was one of things she admired about him. Right now he was wound tighter than an over-coiled spring; his body was rippling with tension. She smoothed a hand over the rigid muscles along his shoulder.

"Talk to me, Ty," she said.

He turned his head, those piercing blue eyes pinning her to the spot. "I'm a moron," he told her. "A beautiful woman asks me to take her home and I...I'm an idiot."

Laughter bubbled up from deep in her stomach, releasing the nerves. Leaning across the table, she picked up the customised glass holding the crème brûlée and, grabbing a spoon, she pierced the hard, sugary coating on top.

A spicy aroma drifted towards her, making her mouth water, but she didn't eat the whole bite. With her eyes on Tyler, she sucked in half the portion and allowed the flavours to coat her tongue.

Oh my god, that's good.

Resisting the urge to close her eyes, she stepped to Tyler and held the spoon out to him. He didn't even hesitate to take her offering. The fact his eyes fluttered shut when the taste hit his senses, made her want to do wicked things to him.

"You can tell Gerard his dessert was a hit," she said, setting the glass on the table. "Now take me home and I might let you feed me the rest."

Laugher bubbled again when he spun to repack the basket. No, he wasn't an idiot, she thought. He was the smartest person she knew.

***

Tyler was grateful for Lilly-May's relaxed chatter on the way back to the car, because he doubted he could form a coherent sentence. He was also grateful she didn't touch him; he had a thin leash on his control. If he didn't know any better, he would suspect their food had been tampered with – the pheromones in the air made his skin burn with the need to take Lilly-May.

He glanced across at her, wondering if she could feel it too. For as long as he could remember he'd wanted her, dreamt of devouring her, inch by delicious inch. Those earlier feelings made him realise how much he had suppressed. They made him wild.

The night had cooled considerably, so he turned up the heat when they finally made it back to the car. Lilly-May had lapsed into silence and this time the space between them was tense – almost suffocating.

"What are you thinking?" Lilly-May asked, eyes on the road ahead.

"I'm not sure you want to know."

Now she turned to him, studying his profile. "Yes, I really do."

Tyler turned briefly to meet her eyes. "I'm thinking I'll go mad if I don't touch you. That I want to kiss every inch of your soft skin and make you ache for me."

He heard her small gasp and couldn't resist another look.

"How fast can this thing go?" she whispered.

Her husky voice made him want to slam his foot on the accelerator and damn the consequences. "Not nearly fast enough."

Her laugh wasn't quite steady. "I'll remind you of that the next time you try to dazzle me with horse power!"

He grinned. "At this rate, I won't be dazzling you with anything. I'll be apologising for my lack of restraint."

"Now you're just teasing," she said, leaning closer. "Put your foot down and show me what you've got."

His next words were practically a growl. "You're killing me."

"Then we're even, because I'm reciting the Highway Code in my head. It's the only reason I haven't crawled into your lap."

His gaze shot to hers and the moment their eyes met their laughter collided. It relieved some of the pressure, though not nearly enough as far as Tyler was concerned.

It was a relief when she sat back, putting some distance between them so he could focus on the road.

The ten minutes to Lilly-May's house felt like the longest in history. He had to force himself to pull the Porsche slowly to the curb, and not mount it.

"Hang on," he said, and stepped out of the car to move around to open her door.

Lilly-May accepted his hand, threading her fingers through his. When she looked into his eyes his heart rate steadied and his pulse levelled out. She was nervous too, but she wanted him. Her desire was real.

Everything seemed to slow; the way they walked casually to the door hand in hand, how he waited for her to find her house keys and let them in. The only light came from a lamp in the narrow hall, but Lilly-May didn't move to hit the light switch.

She turned to face him and the promise in her beautiful green eyes stole his breath. "Kiss me, Ty-"

He bent and covered her mouth, capturing the demand with one of his own. She opened to him without question, her hands bunched in his shirt to pull him closer.

When they broke apart, both breathless, he was surprised that the heat between them no longer flashed and burned. It simmered now, making him want to savour.

As though she read his mind, Lilly-May dropped her hand to take his and, without saying a word, led him down the hall and up the stairs. Only when they were in her bedroom did she let go.

The room wasn't what he'd expected, though the modern, sleek design suited her. He noticed a blend of green and smoky grey around them; with a vanity unit which stretched the length of the main wall. The bed was in the centre of the room, an extravagant affair he couldn't wait to get her into.

When his gaze returned to hers, the green in the décor paled into insignificance compared to the rich shade of her eyes. He reached for her, easing her towards the bed until the backs of her legs brushed against the smooth fabric of the duvet.

He couldn't resist bending his neck to run his lips along her shoulder, feathering hot, wet kisses across her skin. She shuddered, bringing her hands to his shoulders to steady herself. But she didn't explore, she seemed to know what he wanted and understood his need to savour. So he obliged himself, finding the zip at the back of her dress and sliding it down in a slow, sensual movement.

She shivered again, making him smile against her skin. He guided the dress down her body, groaning at the feel of her soft flesh. He stepped back to look at her, his gaze sweeping along her generous curves until he wanted to touch her so much his hands shook.

Lilly-May had other ideas. Her hands shot to his shirt, her fingers not quite steady as they worked the buttons. Tyler didn't help, he was enjoying the feel of her hands too much, especially when she followed his example and swept his shirt over his shoulders and down his arms in a slow, seductive motion.

Her exploration didn't stop there. She smoothed her palms over his pecs, down his stomach and ran her fingertips beneath the waistband of his trousers. It stretched his patience to the limit, yet he allowed her to at least undo his top button before he lost his mind completely and had to take over.

He was about to turn his attention to her body when she grasped his wrists and dragged him down onto the mattress.

"We have all night," she said, laughing as he manoeuvred her higher up the bed. "How about we save the-"

Tyler grinned before he circled her nipple with his tongue. He repeated the action, not because it shut her up – that was merely a side benefit – but because he was intoxicated by the taste of her.

She arched off the bed, threading her fingers into his hair to invite him closer. "Tyler."

It was a sensual whisper which ignited the fire in him, the one that wanted to devour every inch of her. He took his time, enjoying the sound of his name on her lips, and the way her body responded beneath his.

"I'm going to…" she moaned when he ran kisses along her inner thigh. "Get you back for this."

His chuckle vibrated against the apex of her thigh. He knew she felt it from the incoherent sound she made. She was his every teenage fantasy come to life.

"You have no idea how long I've waited for this," he murmured, closing his mouth over her heat. She cried out, tightening her grip in his hair.

Tyler had always prided himself on his patience, but it failed him now. He needed to be inside her, to feel her wrapped around him.

"Thank god," Lilly-May gasped when he moved to reach for his discarded trousers.

She crawled after him, took the condom he was struggling to open, and slid it over his erection, easily the most erotic thing he'd ever experienced. The feel of her hands short-circuited something in his brain. A few seconds later he slid inside her, the deeply satisfied sound of Lilly-May's triumph ringing in his ears. She wrapped herself around him, giving him everything he wanted and so much more as their passion lit up the room.

Later, as Lilly-May lay dozing in his arms, he marvelled at how in tune they were. She'd gotten her own back as she had promised, but it had been the kind of slow, tantalising love making he'd only dreamed of. He felt his chest expand. How could he not tell her everything that was in his heart? He wanted to spend every evening beside her, for the rest of his life.

Because she'd freak out at that level of commitment, that's why.

"I can feel you thinking too hard," she grumbled, making him laugh.

"You know that's not possible, right?"

"So you're not debating about whatever is running through that head of yours?" she asked, snuggling closer.

"I'm happy. That's what I was thinking about." He trailed his fingertips down her arm. "Being with you. It makes me happy." The words that had been circling his head moments ago fell from his lips before he could stop them. "I love you." He tensed, waiting for her to say something, anything. When she didn't he leant back so he could see her face.

She was asleep.

Chapter 8

Lilly-May woke before the alarm. She hated mornings, or at least until she'd had her first coffee and was up to her elbows in dough. But this morning she felt as content as a cat, and just as lazy.

She lay for a few more minutes, enjoying the heavy weight of Tyler's arm across her waist. She couldn't remember the last time someone had spent the night.

You're usually not this easy on a first date.

The thought made her smile. She stretched, rolling gently until she had disentangled herself. She felt the loss immediately. Tyler moaned, turning over in his sleep. He looked so tempting; hair ruffled, long lashes brushing his cheek. His mouth, full and generous, was upturned in a slight smile, and she couldn't help but wonder what he was dreaming about.

Would it be strange between them now? She certainly didn't feel any different, which was odd considering how much their relationship had changed. Her dreams had been of Tyler, telling her that he loved her, and instead of fear, she felt a wave of contentment.

Now, in the light of day, she was afraid of where they were headed. What would happen when the passion burned out? Would they be able to live with the consequences? The last thing she wanted was for him to feel trapped by their history. But then how could she be thinking of love when she had avoided the commitment most of her life? It didn't make any sense.

Pushing aside her niggle of doubt, she padded across the room to the shower.

She usually got to work around 6am, but with the temptation in her bed, she wondered if she might be late this morning. But Tyler was still asleep when she came out of the bathroom, and she didn't have the heart to wake him. Still, she indulged in a little fantasy, the thought of kissing him awake.

Before she could follow through, she dressed quickly and backed out of the bedroom. As she waited for the coffee machine to work its magic, she jotted Tyler a note.

Good morning, Dragon-slayer

I had to go to work, but the coffee should be warm and you can help yourself to anything in the fridge.
Call me when you get this. I want to hear your sexy morning voice. It was hard not to wake you.
Talk soon
LM x

She took her coffee to go, anxious to start her day and work off the jittery nerves which had emerged in the shower.

No sooner had she prepped her work station, her mobile sprang to life on the counter. She snatched it up, a stupid grin on her face when she saw who it was.

"I really wish you'd woken me," Tyler growled in her ear; the best damn morning voice she'd ever heard.

"If I had, it would have made me very late for work." She sighed wistfully. "What time does your shift start?"

"I'm off today. But I have a meeting and then I'll be spending time with Daniel at the hospital."

She heard him stretch, imagined the taught muscles on his chest bunch. "How about you stop by on your way in, and I'll make it up to you?"

He chuckled, making her blush, which was ridiculous. "I think I prefer to wait until we're alone."

"Okay, call me when you get home. I could come over." She began to sort through her ingredients, anything to banish the nerves battling in her stomach.

"I'm counting on it." There was a slight pause as though he were struggling to find the words. "Have a good day, Lilly."

"It'll certainly be an interesting one. I can't seem to lose the goofy smile."

Tyler let out a relieved breath. "Me either. I'll probably get some stick from Daniel."

"Is that a good or a bad thing?"

"Oh it's good," he said, voice low. "Last night was definitely worth it."

She closed her eyes, heart beating like a caged animal in her chest. "I think so too."

They hung up a few minutes later, but it took Lilly-May at least ten to collect her thoughts and start the busy day ahead.

She hardly had a moment to herself for the rest of the morning; she was up to her elbows in orders – literally.

Karen arrived just after twelve, to relieve her in the kitchen. It was an arrangement which worked well; not only did her deputy manager excel in baking their most popular confectionaries, it gave Lilly-May a chance to catch up with the daily visitors. Café 101 generally had three assistants working in front, all of whom were grateful for the extra pair of hands.

Her mobile chimed before she made it out front. It was a message from Tyler.

"Come to the back door."

Lilly-May smiled absently at Karen, and crossed to the exit at the other side of the kitchen. She pushed the door open, peering outside.

"Tyler?" She squealed in surprise when a hand grabbed her wrist and pulled her into the narrow side street. "Whoa-"

She was pressed against the wall of the building before she could form the words. Tyler's mouth was hot and possessive against hers, and she felt the shock waves right down to her toes. She heard voices from the balcony above them, and then everything melted away. Everything except Tyler.

"I changed my mind," he whispered, against her mouth. "I couldn't wait until later."

She sank into him, threading her hands into his hair. "I wanted to wake you this morning. I really wish I had."

"I seem to remember you saying something about making it up to me?" He ran his hands down her body, settling them at her waist to pull her closer.

Lilly-May tilted her hips, teasing a groan out of him. "Oh, I plan to." She met the next kiss with a ferocity of her own, wishing they weren't out in the open.

Tyler ran his thumb across her lips. "You're intoxicating. I want you, Lilly. I can't seem to get enough." His hands tightened. "All I can think about is making love to you, being-"

"This is crazy," she said, panting a little. "If you don't stop we'll be arrested for indecent behaviour."

He buried his face in her neck, his laughter vibrating pleasantly along her skin. "I should let you get back to work, shouldn't I?"

"It is our busiest time," she said, though made no attempt to move.

Tyler was the one to step back. "Until later then." He bent for a sweet kiss which left her breathless.

She watched him jog down the side street, imagined the grin on his face, and groaned. What was happening to her? Tyler had always taken care of his own with a quiet intensity, but now all that passion was focused solely on her she realised how dangerous it was. He made her feel alive in a way she'd never felt before.

"Lilly?"

She jumped guiltily, turning to see Karen in the doorway. "Sorry, I was just…getting a little air."

"Is that what they're calling it these days?" Karen said, stepping back to let Lilly-May into the kitchen. "Is there something you want to tell me?"

Lilly-May bit her lip, failing to hide her smile. "Not yet. I want to savour things for a while." She smoothed her hands over her hair. "And I'm already way too distracted."

She left the kitchen, followed by the sound of Karen's laughter. Stepping behind the counter, she stopped to survey the room; pleased by what she saw. The antique, restored tables, twenty in total, gave the place a rustic feel. Wooden beams ran the length of the café, with hanging globe lights to cast a soft glow. Dylan was a talented architect, and he had gone to town during the renovations. Vibrant reds highlighted the counter and one feature wall, which held artwork by local artists.

Her gaze wandered to the alcove on the far right, honing in on Adrienne. She hadn't realised her friend had stopped by today. She was hunched over her cup, looking a million miles away; alarm bells rang in Lilly-May's head.

It took some juggling, not to mention fast talking, but she made it to Addy's table in under ten minutes.

"Penny for them," she said, slipping into the seat opposite.

Adrienne looked up, her eyes red-rimmed and haunted. "Lucy's sick," she whispered.

"Oh honey." Lilly reached for her hand. "I'm so sorry."

"I don't know how to process it," Adrienne said, squeezing her hand. "We only just found each other. I can't lose her now."

Lilly-May glanced around at the growing crowd. "Why don't we go into my office?"

"I'm okay," Adrienne said, pulling her hand away to reach for her drink. "I just need a minute."

"Anything you want." Lilly-May watched her, at a loss because Addy had boarded herself up behind a tight wall of emotion.

Nearby voices buzzed in Lilly-May's ear. Normally it was a sound she welcomed, but right then it grated. She glanced around, barely registering the fact she had a full house. At least the alcove held some modicum of privacy, though it was adjacent to the metal staircase to the second floor.

"Talk to me, Addy. What's going on?"

Adrienne looked up, met her eyes. Some of the usual spark was back. "She has cancer, has suspected as much for weeks, but didn't let me help her." There was anger in her voice, an emotion she had withheld from her sister. Of that Lilly-May was certain.

She took her hand again. "You've both been through so much. She was probably trying to protect you."

"I know. But I'm not sure she would have told me now if Jamie hadn't pushed the issue, and it hurts."

"Jamie?" Lilly-May frowned. "He knew?"

Adrienne's face softened. "Yes, and he gave her an ultimatum. Tell me or he would."

Lilly-May thought about that. "I think if James knew, then she was already struggling to find a way to tell you. I don't know Lucy well, but I know James and he would have spilled the beans in a heartbeat if he didn't think she would."

Adrienne closed her eyes, taking a deep breath as though to steady herself. "I just want to be there for her." She let go of the breath in a long rush. "And I will be. She starts chemo next week and I'm going with her."

"That's how you get through this. Together." Lilly-May patted their joined hands. "If there's anything you need. I'm here."

"Thanks, Lilly. I-" Adrienne broke off when a shadow fell across the table.

They both turned to see Sebastian enter the alcove, with Dylan a step behind. There was one thing the Davies boys excelled at, and that was coming together in a crisis.

Lilly-May watched, a smile on her lips as Adrienne got up to step into Sebastian's waiting arms. The display of affection wasn't out of place in such a busy environment, but they turned heads all the same.

"Want to head home?" Sebastian asked.

Adrienne stepped back with a small smile. "Maybe we should. I'm keeping Lilly from her work."

"That's my job," Dylan quipped, brushing past Sebastian to get in on the action. He hugged Adrienne. "Take my brother home for lunch. He works too hard." He leant to whisper something in Adrienne's ear, which had her tearing up again.

She ran an affectionate hand down his arm before turning to Lilly-May. "I'll call you later."

Sebastian squeezed Lilly's shoulder. His blue eyes, so much like Tyler's, held hers. "Kick him out when he becomes too much of a distraction," he said, glancing at Dylan who had slid into Adrienne's vacant spot. "Behave yourself." Rolling his eyes at Dylan's innocent expression, Sebastian took Adrienne's hand and led her out.

"So..." Dylan said.

Lilly-May narrowed her eyes. "Here I am thinking good thoughts and you didn't come here to offer Addy moral support, did you?"

"Blah, blah, blah," Dylan said in a bored tone. "Just spill it."

She held out for all of ten seconds before the laughter erupted. Dressed in a tailored suit, with his dark good looks, and athletic build, Dylan was an attractive man. When he smiled he was lethal. Lilly-May was glad they were mostly out of sight so they didn't draw too much unwanted attention. He was an outrageous flirt, and couldn't help himself.

"Isn't there some rule about not going into detail about your brother's love life?"

Dylan whistled long and low. Luckily the place was packed so the sound barely registered. "You work fast, Lilly-pot." His chuckle was positively wicked. "I want details."

"Ew," she said, pulling a face. "You're my best friend, but there are some limits."

He gave a long suffering sigh. "At least tell me that my little brother didn't let the side down."

Lilly-May stood, biting her lip to hide the smile. "You're insufferable," she said, leaning close so nobody could overhear. "But it was the best sex of my life."

He hadn't expected her to answer. He enjoyed pushing her buttons and making her laugh. To see the surprise shining in his goofy expression just about made her day. If Tyler hadn't done that already.

"Now. I have a job to do, so come keep me company and stop fishing for information you don't really want." She walked away and left him staring after her.

By the time she'd made it back to the counter, Dylan had recovered and was back to his charming self.

***

Daniel was entertaining the nursing staff when Tyler arrived, or more accurately, trying to work his charm so he could get out earlier. He was getting stronger, a fact which worked in his favour because the doctor had promised him a pass to Grayson's funeral in two days.

"How's the head?" Tyler asked, surprised they were alone.

"Still attached." Daniel pulled a face. "I can't believe you came empty handed. Do you have any idea how bored I am in this place?"

Tyler looked pointedly at the play station on the unit beside him, and the other goodies a stream of well-wishers brought on a regular basis. "They were out of grapes."

"Then tell me something to take my mind off these four walls. Seriously, man, I'm losing my sense of humour here."

Tyler snorted. "If the ceiling coming down on your head can't do that, then your funny bone can handle a little boredom."

"Ha. Don't quit your day job." Daniel's eyes were grave now. "I miss him, Ty. Every damn day. I can't get what happened out of my head."

"I know. We all feel it. But we have to move on somehow, because it's what he would have wanted." Tyler stretched his legs out in front of him. "I've been thinking of doing something for him, you know, in his memory. Something we can all invest in."

Daniel perked up. "Like what?"

"I'm not sure, but I started thinking about everything he did for the community. How he fought to make things better when he had such a shitty start in life." Grayson had been an orphan, had moved through the foster system and faced hardship every step of the way, yet he had never lost his faith in people.

"I think it's a great idea," Daniel said, his voice thick with emotion. "And it's just want we all need. Something we can do together."

"Then I'll think on it, and we can throw some ideas around." He stood to pour himself a glass of coke from Daniel's stash. "How's Katie? I expected her to be here."

"She had to go back to work." Daniel smiled. "But I'm surprised she's not here already. I swear she thinks I'll disappear if she leaves for a second."

Tyler dipped his glass towards the bed. "Like you don't enjoy the attention."

"There's nothing like the love of a…" Daniel's voice trailed off. He narrowed his eyes on Tyler's face. "What's that look?"

"What?" He tried his hardest to hold back the smile, but couldn't do it. "I don't have any look."

"Bullshit." Daniel considered for a moment, his eyes growing wide. "You got laid." The smile, which had been working its way up his face, retreated again. "Tell me you didn't fall into Lorna's bed again."

Tyler was about to reply, but his friend was shaking his head. He wanted to tell him to stop.

"No, not Lorna. You wouldn't have that goofy, puppy dog...shit, you had sex with Lilly-May."

"Christ, does everyone in Winchester know about-"

"Stop evading. I'm right aren't? You finally did it, you finally grew a pair."

Tyler laughed. "I'm going to ignore that, since it's not polite to hit an injured man." The smile broke free. "But it just so happens that I went on a date with her last night."

Daniel wagged a finger at him. "You did more than go on a date, but I'll not split hairs. That's great, Ty. Grayson would have been stoked."

It sobered them a little. "The moment I got to the station this morning I wished I could tell him. I would have taken the riling, just for the chance to share it with him."

"My Katie would say he knows, and that he's happy for you." Daniel grinned. "But you're right. He would have given you some serious shit over this one, and told you not to mess it up."

They were silent for a minute or two, then a nurse came in to check on Daniel. Tyler lost himself in thoughts of Lilly-May, of spending the evening with her.

"I can't believe you were holding out on me," Daniel said, when they were alone again. "Do you want to satisfy a sick man's curiosity?"

"You've got the sick man part right."

Daniel roared with laughter. "Now that was funny. What are you doing sitting here with me when you could be with her?"

"I was just asking myself the same thing." Tyler downed the coke. "But I'll take pity on you a while longer."

He actually stayed two hours, and only left because other visitors arrived. Despite the camaraderie, he knew his friend was covering pain under the humour. He might be getting stronger, but it would be a while before he returned to work and Daniel needed his family to get through the tough days ahead.

He told Lilly-May about their conversation later that night, as they lay on the couch, catching up on their days. She told him about Adrienne, and about his brother, fishing for information. It felt so right he was tempted to confess everything again, this time when she was awake.

"I didn't know about Grayson's family. Losing them so young, that must have been tough," she said, playing with the buttons on his shirt.

"He didn't remember them, but I guess they left an impression. He was one of the kindest people I know." Tyler looked down at her hands, amused to realise she had unbuttoned half his shirt.

"What'll happen at the funeral?" she asked, her hands making light work of her task.

"I imagine half the town will be there. Grayson made an impression on everyone." He closed his eyes when she slid a hand across his bare chest. "Are you trying to distract me?"

"Is it working?" she asked, leaning to run her lips over the path her hand had just taken.

"Hmm." He laughed when she poked him in the ribs.

"I can't seem to keep my hands off you for two minutes." She soothed the jab with a kiss. "What'll happen when we're with friends and family and I'm lusting after you?"

He wanted to laugh at the term, but he heard the worry behind the question. "Are you asking if we should keep this a secret?"

She sat up, looking at him. "I think keeping it a secret is going to be hard considering Dylan's big mouth, but do you want to be…open about it?"

"I think we should do whatever comes naturally." He cupped her chin with his hand. "Like you said, this is new to us, so maybe we should take things slow." It wasn't what he wanted to say. If it were up to him he would make it clear to everyone she was his. But he didn't want to rush her. He didn't want to put her in a position where she would feel uncomfortable around those she relied on.

"It does feel natural, doesn't it?" she whispered. "What's happening between us?"

"The most natural thing in the world." He drew her down for a kiss, lingering, drawing in the taste of her.

They undressed each other slowly, fumbling because they didn't have much room, despite the size of the couch. When they tumbled to the floor, laughing, that felt natural too.

Tyler made love to her on the thick rug in the centre of his living room. His tastes had always been modest, but he was glad he had invested in such a luxurious item. It became his favourite thing about the space.

Neither of them wanted to move, content to sleep, wrapped around one another. But at some point, Tyler lifted her back to the couch, and used a blanket to cover them.

He lay awake for a while, thinking about her question. There was no way he could hide his feelings from his family. He couldn't go back, not now. Every time he looked at her, he fell a little bit more. He hadn't thought it possible. It scared him because he didn't know how he would ever go back to being her friend. He would simply have to convince her that they belonged together. That the connection between them was beyond the physical she felt right now, and spoke of a love so large and bright – it was a fire that would never die.

Chapter 9

The sight of Tyler saying goodbye to his friend, surrounded by the men and women from the fire service, and what felt like the entire community, would stay with Lilly-May for a long time.

She wanted to go to him, to stand beside him, but she didn't know how to put the desire into words and this day was about Grayson, about saying goodbye and celebrating the man he had been. So she stood, side by side with Tyler's family, and James who had flown in for the day, and watched over him.

The wake took place at the station, and was a community affair. Lilly-May had given Tyler his privacy, finding only a moment to place her hand in his and let him know she was there.

Because it was what they did, Veronica and Simon held a family party later that night, and everyone was there to stay, including Adrienne and Sebastian, though they had disappeared to the cottage to put Elijah to bed. Connie had volunteered for the role of babysitter.

As they all gathered on the custom made veranda, Lilly-May sat at Dylan's feet, she wished she could go to Tyler and wrap her arms around him. She didn't care who saw, or what they thought. But he wanted to take things slowly, so she would respect his wishes. It wasn't that she didn't agree. She already had doubts about their ability to go back, so, although being with him didn't feel wrong, it would hurt them both if she involved the whole family.

She knew she was caught up in the passion she felt, the hunger he had awoken. It still confused her, made her wonder where it had been hiding, and how those feelings could become all consuming, so quickly.

"I think Gray would have gotten a kick out of that send-off," Chris told Tyler, throwing an arm around his neck. "His family did him proud."

"As did mine," Tyler said, tipping his glass towards the centre of the group. "I couldn't have gotten though this day without you. Any of you."

"You know what we need right now?" James said, looking from Tyler to Adrienne. "We need one of Derek's ditties."

"Or an Ode," Dylan piped up. "Do you remember when we christened your patio, Seb?"

Adrienne giggled, leaning to Sebastian to murmur something only he could hear.

"Do you want to share with the rest of us?" Lilly-May asked, then pointed at Addy and Sebastian. "Not you two. I think we can figure that out."

James leant forward in his seat and caught Lilly-May's eye. "Our brother loved to make up ditties when we were kids, especially about Addy," he said, smiling at the memory.

"I was remembering that the day the boys finished Seb's patio," Adrienne continued smoothly.

Tyler decided to get in on the action. "You know how D likes to celebrate his successes by marking the occasion," he said, his gaze encompassing the group. "Well, Addy did the honours with an Ode to an Architect."

"Perhaps you should say something, Ty. You know, one Dragon-slayer to another," James suggested.

"Actually, this might be the perfect time to give you this," Lilly-May cut in, rising to retrieve a small rose plant she'd hidden beneath a chair. She had chosen the colour, a glorious flame orange as a symbol of friendship. "Since you enjoy to help V with her garden, I thought it would be a nice addition. A reminder of Grayson." She thrust it towards him. "To family."

In a smooth motion, Chris stepped forward to take Tyler's glass and the plant.

Without missing a beat Tyler pulled Lilly-May against him and enveloped her in a hug. "Thank you," he whispered. "It's perfect."

Lilly-May smiled against his chest. "What do you say we go plant it?"

It was Chris who answered, when Tyler remained silent. "Excellent idea." He slapped Tyler on the back. "Come on, bro. I know just the spot."

Finally loosening his hold, Tyler looked her in the eye, his blue eyes shining bright with emotion. He opened his mouth to speak, but the moment was broken as the others gathered.

"It's beautiful, Lilly," Adrienne said, running a hand down her arm.

"It is, isn't it?" Her eyes flickered to the rose, then back to Tyler. She wished they were alone, was overwhelmed with a need to have him all to herself.

Before she could analyse that too deeply, she was whisked away in the excitement of the group. They gathered their glasses, and crossed the grounds, following Chris until they reached the main garden.

Veronica had laid out the tools they needed for the planting ceremony, a fact which made Lilly-May smile. She stood with the others, waiting patiently as Tyler knelt to prepare the soil, handling the rose with care before lowering it into its new home.

"Okay, my man," James said, stepping up beside Tyler to hand him his glass. "It's over to you."

Tyler took the offering, raising his hand, and his voice. "To Grayson. My friend. A man with a heart of fire. May his light burn like an eternal flame."

"Amen to that," James said, tapping his glass against Tyler's.

Lilly-May swallowed the lump in her throat, moving with the others to share a toast.

Two hours later, Lilly-May found herself in a guest room in the main house. She was wide awake, partly because of the wine she had drunk, but mostly because her thoughts were on Tyler.

Closing her eyes, she listened to the sounds of the house. All was quiet. She worked out the route to Tyler's old room in her head, and wondered if she could make it undetected.

"Only one way to find out," she whispered, clapping a hand over her mouth when a laugh tried to break free.

She crept out of bed, stopping at the full length mirror beside the dressing table. The long t-shirt she'd had since college was hardly the most seductive outfit, but he might not notice in the dark. She ran her hands through her hair, tidying it as best she could, before stepping away from her reflection.

Out in the hall, she crept across the carpeted floor, pausing at the top of the stairs to listen for sounds below. She heard nothing and continued, eyes on each door she passed, and ears alert.

She had to pause halfway to Tyler's door to get her breath. She hadn't realised she'd been holding it, but when laughter bubbled in her throat at the image she made, her lungs protested. As she continued she was hit with a powerful memory, one she hadn't thought about in a long time.

It was the night of her graduation and Veronica had thrown a party in her honour. Tyler was just finishing college, so he must have been eighteen. He had been distant that night, she remembered. But when she'd tried to talk to him, he'd left the party abruptly and holed himself up in his room. She couldn't recall their conversation, but something about it niggled at her. It had that night too, because she'd snuck up to his room and debated with herself about confronting him.

Lilly-May reached towards the door handle, past and present merging as she hesitated before turning the cold metal. Sheets rustled inside the room, and she wondered if he could sense her. The idea blew away her indecision and she turned the handle, pushing the door wide.

There was a lamp on beside the bed, casting a shadow across Tyler's naked chest. He was sitting up, eyes on her, and what she read in his expression made her toes curl against the thick carpet.

"Close the door," he whispered when she continued to stand, half in and half out.

Lilly-May let out a slow breath, holding his gaze as she closed the door at her back. He didn't say anything else, simply continued to eat her up with his intense gaze, until her body tingled in response.

She wondered if he was thinking about the night of her party, because she had thought of little else. To break the tension - or perhaps amplify it - she clasped the hem of her t-shirt and pulled it over her head. She was naked now, yet felt no vulnerability. Not when he looked at her like she was the most beautiful woman he had ever seen.

She heard him swallow, watched his eyes drop to her breasts, lingering before moving down her body. "This is a dream," he said, voice thick with longing. "It has to be."

With a small smile, she crossed the room to climb onto the bed. Crawling slowly towards him, the smile grew when he pushed back the covers to reveal he wasn't wearing anything either.

She put a hand on his chest to push him back against the pillows, positioning herself so they were skin to skin.

"Lilly."

She kissed his next words into her mouth, smoothing her hands across his face. "This is better than any dream," she whispered, running her tongue along his lower lip.

Tyler groaned, his hands possessive as they roamed her body. "I don't know about that," he said, in a breathless tone. "At this rate I'll only last thirty seconds."

"Me too." Her laugh was playful as she sat up to straddle him.

His hands went to her hips. "I have a-"

Lilly-May shook her head. "Not tonight." Her gaze dropped to his body, all but vibrating in its need for her. "I've taken care of it."

She lifted her hips, smiling wickedly when he took her weight. She smoothed her hand along the hard length of him, finding pleasure in his sharp intake of breath, in the way his blue eyes flashed to hers.

"Lilly," he said again, a quiet plea she answered by taking him into her with excruciating slowness.

He slipped his hands beneath her thighs, lifting her slightly so he could sit up to hook her legs around him. The position sent him deeper, and pleasure rolled through her body in a wave. She would have cried out, lost in the feel of him, but he wrapped his arms around her and kissed her; drawing out the sensation. He was relentless, pushing her to the very edge of reason, only to calm the storm with gentle caresses, which tested her control.

He seemed to know her body's every desire, sensed immediately when she had reached her limit. Flipping her onto her back, he wound his fingers through hers and let himself go.

Lilly-May awoke just before dawn to find herself alone in Tyler's bed. She wondered briefly if he was in the shower, but couldn't hear the water running.

Giving herself a minute to get her bearings she climbed out of bed and walked to the chair in front of the desk. Her t-shirt was hanging over the back, so Tyler had picked it up before he left.

A dozen questions ran through her head, followed by scenes of their love making. Had it been too real for him? Was he regretting the intimacy they had shared?

"Get a grip," she chastised herself, pulling the t-shirt over her head on her way to the door.

She opened it a crack, horrified at the prospect of doing the walk of shame and bumping into Veronica, or worse – Simon.

There was no sign of anyone in the hall, so she dashed out, trying not to run on her way back to the guest room. Once there she showered quickly, pulled her wet hair into a pony tail and throwing on the first outfit she found.

She made it to the bottom of the staircase when Tyler emerged carrying a tray. His smile was relaxed and easy.

It's only you who's freaking out.

"I was just bringing you breakfast in bed," he said, waving the tray.

Lilly-May eyes went to the limp toast, the glass of orange, and mug of coffee. She snagged the coffee and brought it to her lips.

After a long sip she worked up a smile for him. "This is great."

He watched her, a slight frown creasing his brow. "Do you want to take it into the kitchen?"

"Great idea. Anywhere the coffee is on tap. I'm feeling out of sorts this morning." She put a hand on his arm before stepping past. Her heart was beating a mile a minute, it was a wonder the whole house didn't hear.

What the hell is wrong with me?

"Talk to me, Lilly," Tyler said, when they entered the kitchen. He put the tray on the nearest counter and turned to face her.

"I'm okay, Ty, I promise. It's just…I don't know. It was a long day yesterday."

He frowned again, making her feel guilty for killing his mood. "Is this about last night?" he asked.

"Of course not."

Liar.

"I came to you, remember?" She walked over to grab the plate from the tray. "Maybe I'm still adjusting to our new…situation."

His brows rose. "That's an interesting way of putting it." He used her delaying tactics; removing the orange and replacing the tray on the rack. "You would tell me if you're having second thoughts?" he said, so casually it was her turn to frown.

She forced a light laugh. "Will you listen to us? This doesn't feel very natural does it? Let's not do the awkward thing. I've already had my walk of shame this morning."

Tyler grinned, relaxing again. "Now there's an interesting idea."

"What are you two cooking up?" Chris asked, sauntering into the kitchen. His gaze dropped to the plate in Lilly-May's hand. "Not much. Clearly!"

She laughed, turning her face when he bent to kiss her cheek. "Did you move in? Every time I see you lately, you're here."

Chris dropped his voice in a conspiratorial whisper. "I'm their favourite. Mom and pops like having me around."

He had always referred to Veronica and Simon that way. His own parents didn't take offense, or they wouldn't if they stopped in one place long enough to pay attention.

"I hate to break it to you," Tyler said. "But they only keep you for your culinary skills."

Chris laughed good-naturedly. "Speaking of which, I'd better get this show on the road. Jamie's plane leaves in a few hours."

"In that case, I'll leave you to set up and go round up the troops. My nephew should have the whole cottage up by now."

Lilly-May almost sighed with relief when he'd gone. She had too many thoughts, too many confusing emotions, and being around him only made it worse. "What can I do to help?" she asked Chris, walking to retrieve her coffee.

"How about whipping up some pancakes?" he suggested, moving swiftly from cupboard to cupboard to gather supplies.

"I'm on it."

They worked side by side for the next thirty minutes, both content in their task. Lilly-May managed to find her centre again, so when the family crowded into the room, she began to wonder what all the fuss was about.

Chapter 10

Tyler walked James to the car, trying to find the words to express how much their friendship meant to him.

"If you say thank you one more time, I swear to god I'm going to throttle you," James said, putting his overnight bag in the boot.

Tyler ignored him. "It meant a lot you were here."

"It goes without saying. We're family, Ty, and family look out for each other." He narrowed his eyes. "Is everything okay?"

"Yes. No…I don't know." Tyler leant against the rental, glancing at the house. "Things were a little…intense last night, and I think Lilly is freaking out."

James slapped a hand to his shoulder. "She's adjusting. You went from 0 to 60 in the blink of an eye, so it shouldn't be a surprise."

"Do you think I should slow down a little? Take a step back?"

"I think you should give yourself a break. You buried your feelings so deep I'm surprised you didn't declare-" James stopped when he caught Tyler's discomfort. "You told her you're in love with her? No wonder she's freaking out."

"Gee, thanks." He grinned. "And I sort of told her…I just didn't know she was asleep at the time."

"Christ! That sounds like some cheesy scene from-"

"You're going to miss your flight," Adrienne said, walking to them with long, sure strides.

James slung an arm around her neck and kissed the top of her head. "Relax, I've still got time." His eyes met Tyler's. "Hang in there, man. She couldn't keep her eyes off you yesterday, so that's got to count for something."

Tyler wasn't sure about that. He didn't doubt their chemistry; a spark which threatened to consume them both. But when the fire died down, what then? Would there be anything left to salvage?

"Am I missing something?" Adrienne asked, looking from one to the other.

James winked at Tyler. "Only a failed declaration, some serious action and a major freak-out. No big deal."

Tyler laughed, the sound drowned out by Adrienne's cackle of amusement.

"I'll unpick that later," she said, her gaze swinging from Tyler to James. "But while we're on the subject of communication…why are you avoiding Lucy?"

"Ouch!" Tyler whistled long and low. "Bonus points for a nice segue," he added, holding his palm towards Adrienne. He dropped it when he caught James' scowl.

"I'm not avoiding her, I just figured you guys had a lot to talk about."

Adrienne wasn't letting him off the hook that easily. "She needs you too, Jamie."

"What do you want from me?" James asked, taking a step back. "I got her to come clean, and now she has support."

Tyler, adept at stepping between them when a fight was brewing, cleared his throat. "She'll get more support than she bargained for now the Davies clan are involved."

"Okay, okay," Adrienne said, moving to cup James' face in her hands so she could kiss his cheek. When she released him, she repeated the steps with Tyler. "I love you guys, and I swear you were separated at birth." She shook her head. "You'd both slay dragons to protect your family, and yet you're unaware of your true strength."

Tyler flicked the end of her nose. "If you're going to lecture us, Jamie will definitely miss his plane."

"You were always better at this stuff," James said, voice gruff. "But I'll call her, okay."

"Okay." She grinned. "As long as you stop hiding and promise to come home soon."

James groaned, putting his hands loosely around Adrienne's neck. "If you don't give me a break, I'll be hiding your body."

"Wouldn't do you any good," Adrienne said, laughing. "I'd come back to haunt you. There's no getting rid of me." She hugged him, eyes dancing as she looked at Tyler over James' shoulder. "And we've never been able to shake that one."

Tyler stepped forward, smiling at the familiarity of the scene. He made an 'aw' sound and opened his arms wide, knowing James would duck out of the way.

"I'm going," James muttered. "Before this shit gets any more intense."

"Have a safe flight," Adrienne said, linking her arm through Tyler's.

James nodded. "Later."

They watched him drive away, letting the silence settle around them when they could no longer hear the roar of the engine.

"How are you holding up?" Tyler asked, nudging her gently with his shoulder.

"Honestly?" She smiled. "I'm scared out of my mind." Her head dropped onto his shoulder. "But I'm not giving up. I'm going to help her fight this."

"Of course you are." He smiled when she looked up. "What are your plans today?" She had taken a rare morning off from the breakfast show, and although Tyler understood she had done it for him, he also knew the time would do her good.

"Dylan is taking us sailing," she said, visibly shaking off her mood. "I actually came looking for you. I was hoping you'd to join us."

"That sounds great." He bent to kiss her cheek. "Give me five minutes, okay?"

She nodded. "See you back at the house."

Tyler turned, stepping onto the path which led to the garden. He thought of his brother's yacht, a vessel Dylan had named after their mother. His lips curved at the idea of spending a day on the water.

The smile deepened as he recalled the last time he'd been aboard the Veronica. He had convinced Dylan to let him take her out, and Grayson had found his sea legs the hard way. It was a good memory, one he could take out and savour because it was the day they cemented their friendship.

He sat on a bench beside his mother's rose garden, and looked at the new addition to the carefully cultured display. The sunlight danced along the bright orange petals, casting a glow which brought the plant to life – a living flame.

"I miss you, buddy," he said, appreciating the true meaning of Lilly-May's gift. It brought him closer to his friend, gave him a chance to share his thoughts.

"I wish you were here to ride me about the mess I'm making. You always understood me, why I can't risk losing Lilly-May." He bowed his head, frustrated with himself. "I'm scared, Gray. I'm scared of what happens when the fire burns out." He laughed, feeling foolish.

"I guess I don't want her to feel cut off from the family, you know, if things end badly. They're so great." Tyler glanced back at the rose. "They keep thinking of ways to offer their support, small things like taking me sailing because they know we had fun together at sea." He laughed again. "They don't know how much fun, or about the accident."

It hadn't been entirely their fault, although they had agreed to the impromptu party in the first place. A celebration which almost ended in disaster. Tyler had taken his watchful eye from the group for only a minute, and one of Stevie's friends, a prankster with a wild streak, had put on a show. The fact Tom became the spectacle by falling overboard, cooled his jets considerably, and he learnt a valuable lesson.

When they had fished him out of the sea, regulated his temperature and checked for injuries, Tyler had been ready to put the drama to bed. But Grayson had other ideas. He gave Tom a lecture on safety, on responsibility, and then called an end to the party. Later, as they cleaned up, Grayson had demonstrated to Tyler how the trick was supposed to go down, balancing atop the hand rail with his usual aplomb. It had ended the day as it begun – with laughter.

"I wonder what D would say if I climbed the handrail?" Tyler said, and he could almost hear Grayson's response.

He looked up at the sound of footsteps, surprised when he spotted Lilly-May. "I thought you left," he said, rising.

"The boss gave me the morning off." She chuckled, taking a step closer. "And by boss, I mean Sebastian."

"Does that mean you're joining us?" He knew she enjoyed sailing, had accompanied Dylan many times. It was easy to picture Lilly-May aboard the yacht; hair blowing in the breeze, eyes bright with laughter.

She held out a hand. "Absolutely."

Tyler was struck by a barrage of memories, something James might call a sequence, because of the way they played out in his head. All the times Lilly-May had reached for his hand, sought him out, or pulled him into conversation. It was one of the reasons he cherished their friendship, and he prayed to god they wouldn't lose that connection.

He put his hand in hers, revelling in the familiarity. "Thank you for my gift, Lilly," he said, glancing over his shoulder. "You know me so well." If he hadn't turned back to her then, he might have missed the flicker of doubt. "What is it?"

"Nothing." She shook her head. "It just scares me sometimes, thinking of you as my lover. It makes me question what I know..." Her voice trailed off.

"So that's what this morning was all about?" Tyler dropped her hand so he could cup her face. "You've always seen me, Lilly. Always. But this side of me is bound to be different. It's a level of intimacy that only comes with being my lover." He bent to brush his lips against hers. "Perhaps what scares you, is not that it's unknown, but that it feels like an extension of what we've always had."

"I'm overthinking it, aren't I?" she whispered.

"You're not the only one guilty of that. I'm terrified of what will happen if we screw this up."

She laughed, wrapping her arms around him to rest her head against his heart. "Then we should both let go of the history, and live in the here and now."

"Now there's an idea." When she lifted her head, he captured her mouth in a slow, sweet kiss, which was full of promise. "I just wish the here and now was a little more private."

Her eyes shone with amusement when they looked into his. "I'm starting to think you really are only interested in my body." She stepped back and slipped her hand in his again. "Let's go sailing, Ty. There's nothing stopping us from sneaking into one of the cabins. It might be an adventure."

Tyler groaned. He didn't know about adventure, it sounded more like torture. If he had his own vessel he could christen every cabin with her, make love to her under the stars and spend the night in her arms. But it wasn't his vessel, and he would have to temper his desire, resist touching her until they were in private. It was enough to drive him mad.

"You have an evil streak," he muttered as they walked back toward the house.

Lilly-May glanced at him with a wicked smile. "Someone very wise pointed out that we have a lot to learn about each other." She stopped on the path to the front door. "I happen to enjoy delayed gratification, and," she trailed a finger down his chest. "You haven't seen anything yet."

Tyler watched her walk away, knowing the provocative sway of her hips was designed to make him suffer, and yet all he felt was simple joy. She was playing with him, which meant she was no longer hung up on doubt. He planned to take full advantage of that.

Chapter 11

Tyler was having a bad day. The investigators had found evidence linking the arson to three other fires and, based on the one they were currently fighting, she made it number four.

He had missed the signs before, but this time he felt it in the air. She was unreasonably angry, burning too bright too quickly and the building wasn't empty. If things went badly, the arsonist would be adding murder to the mix.

The air was thick with smoke and fear. They all knew they were running out of time. As Tyler pushed his way forward, towards the last door in the old office building, he thought about what lay on the other side.

There would be no warning rattle, no time to prepare. The heat was another thing entirely. He could sense it pressing outward, could imagine the flames – like a serpents tongue, licking up the walls as they prepared to strike. But they had to check every floor, search every room.

An explosion lifted Tyler off his feet and sent him barrelling against the adjacent wall. He rolled over, fighting the suffocating effect of claustrophobia and checked his men. His Watch Manager barked in his earpiece, which wouldn't have worried him, except for the fact he was speaking a foreign tongue. Tyler didn't understand a word.

He shook his head to clear it. The smoke circled, drifting over his body in a long, lazy roll. The detected movement from the corner of his eye and forced his focus back. A burly man staggered into view, with a towel wrapped around his face and a blanket draped carelessly over his shoulders.

Tyler saw two of his colleagues intercept the man, who gestured to the room behind him. His legs had turned to rubber but he pushed forward. The second explosion took him off his feet again, and this time he was tempted to stay down.

Of course he got back up, putting one foot in front of the other as he followed the path of least resistance. Outside he fell to his knees, pulling the mask from his face to draw in a large breath. He felt dizzy; a result of the fall, coupled with his anger toward the person responsible for such mindless destruction.

Blinking away the spots in his vision, he did a quick roll call to make sure everyone was out. As he waited, he watched a small bird circle, the orange strip on its wing reminding him of the burning tip of a flame.

Get a grip, Ty.

He tried to stand, but his legs weren't quite steady, and a paramedic caught him with strong sure hands.

"Why don't you take a load off for a minute?" Jenkins asked.

Their paths had crossed more than once, and he knew the man wouldn't take any shit. "I might just sit down a while." He allowed Jenkins to lead him to the back of the ambulance and lowered himself onto the step.

It wasn't until he got his breath back that he realised they had company: a news crew and at least a dozen people milling behind a barrier his crew had erected.

"What's all this?" he muttered, suddenly glad he could hide out for a minute.

"Word got out about the arsonist and someone phoned this in. I guess having a famous brother will ramp up the ratings," Jenkins said, snapping into action when his colleague called.

"Shit," Tyler muttered, then spotted Lorna rushing towards him. "Shit."

"Tyler, thank god you're okay," she cried, loud enough to turn heads.

"I'm fine. Just needed a minute." He softened when she sat down beside him, because he saw genuine fear in her eyes. "What are you doing here, Lorna?"

She blushed, turning to look at the news van. "I've been dating an anchor at the local station and we were…together when the news came in."

He stared at her, genuinely surprised. "I hope you're not the reason they're sniffing around."

Lorna grabbed his arm, her eyes pleading. "They knew about the fires, I don't know how, but they knew, I swear. But I might have mentioned you were Gray's best friend and they got excited that one of the-"

"Davies family is involved," he finished. He couldn't be angry with her, not really. The name had brought attention in some form or another his whole life. "Just be careful, Lorna. I don't want to see you get hurt." It was the truth. He had treated her badly and she didn't deserve it.

"Thanks, Ty," she said, resting her head against his shoulder. "I know what I'm doing."

He looked toward the onlookers, wondering if the arsonist was among them, and froze when he found himself looking into a familiar sea green.

What the hell?

Lilly-May was furious. He could see it in the firm set of her jaw, the tight lines around her eyes. He couldn't understand what had her so worked up, but then her gaze slid to Lorna and he knew.

Pain seared across his chest at the look of betrayal on her face.

He didn't follow her when she turned and fled. He couldn't. He had a job to do. "I'd better get back to work," he said to Lorna.

She sat up, smiling. "Maybe I could stop by the station later?"

He rose to hold out a hand for her. "We'd like that. Don't be a stranger, okay?" He took a step forward and then turned back. "And if you ever need us, we'll be there in a heartbeat. We're family."

As he walked away he considered the picture they made in the back of the ambulance. It hurt that Lilly-May didn't trust him, but considering all he knew about her, he wondered if he could blame her. He had been keeping a pretty big secret, and based on her reaction today, it was time to lay his cards on the table.

***

Lilly-May kept him waiting on the doorstep so long he began to wonder if she would answer. He knew she was in because her car was in the drive, and when he'd called her mobile, he heard the ring.

He'd considered bringing flowers, but that made him look guilty when he had nothing to apologise for, so he'd arrived empty handed.

"I don't want to talk to you right now, Tyler," Lilly-May said, through the door. Her tone sent a chill through him.

"Open the damn door, Lilly. This is ridiculous."

The door flew open before he'd finished. "What's ridiculous is you cosying up to someone else only hours after leaving my bed." Her eyes were red, and the evidence of her tears made him angry all over again.

"Will you listen to yourself?" he said, storming past her without being invited. "Do you know anything about me?"

"I thought I did," she snapped, slamming the door. "Nothing makes sense anymore. I don't even know why I went to Castle Park, but I heard the sirens and…" Her voice trailed off.

He thought they were past this, had almost believed they could set aside the history, the baggage they both carried. But the insecurities which had followed them into the relationship, now threatened to tear them apart.

He drew in a calming breath. "And what, Lilly?"

"I started thinking about how much you've lost on the job and the next thing I know I'm following the sound of the siren and freaking out because you were in that building and…then there you were and I was so relieved, but-"

"Take a breath," he instructed, wanting to reassure her, even knowing she wouldn't allow it. "Lorna is just a friend."

"A friend you've never mentioned?"

He ground his teeth. "You've never shown an interest in my work before, otherwise you might-"

"That's because you shut me out. Jesus, Tyler, for the past few years you've barely said a thing about your personal life."

"That's not true." He didn't convince either of them. "We talk all the time."

Lilly-May walked to the couch and flopped onto it with a sigh. "So why didn't I know about your friend?"

He resented the way she said the word, like it was something seedy. "It never came up."

She rolled her eyes. "So there's never been anything between you?"

Tyler opened his mouth and then closed it again. She had him there, but how did he describe his relationship with Lorna without making the situation worse?

"I'm not sure we have the same definition of friendship," she murmured, the words distorted behind her hands.

"It was a mistake, a…error in judgement."

Way to make it better, Ty.

Lilly-May dropped her hands, her expression blank. "You seem to be doing that a lot lately."

He wanted to tell her that was unfair, and realised how it had sounded. "Lilly, listen to me. I know I'm not explaining this very well, but there's nothing between me and Lorna. There never was." The doubt on her face added fuel to the fire. He didn't have anything to feel guilty about. Damn it. "For god's sake, she looks like you. Can't you understand what that means?"

She stood so quickly he took an involuntary step back. "That's supposed to make me feel better? You didn't have the nerve to go after the real thing so you settled for a substitute?" She stepped towards him. "You think I want to be someone's obsession?"

"Obsession?" He wanted to laugh at that, how pathetic it made him. He'd been such a fool. "I guess that says it all, doesn't it?" He turned towards the door. "I'd call it love, and maybe I was a coward for not telling you sooner, but maybe I was trying to protect us from this."

He didn't wait for her response, he'd heard enough. It had been a mistake to think she would understand. Where Lilly-May was concerned, his timing had always been off.

***

Lilly-May sank into the couch, feeling numb from the confrontation with Tyler. He loved her? How could she have missed that, and what the hell was she going to do about it? She had overreacted to seeing him with another woman, she knew that, but she hadn't been able to rationalise her feelings. She'd been on a roller-coaster since he'd kissed her, and that was before he'd confessed to loving her.

Dylan's words came back to her, the morning after their party. Had he known, she wondered. Had she been the only one to miss it?

She hit her head against the cushions, wishing she had someone to talk to. Adrienne was her closest friend besides Dylan, but she couldn't go to either. Adrienne had enough on her plate, and Tyler's brother was hardly a good sounding board right now.

"Damn it," she muttered, hitting her head again, harder this time. She had always gone to Dylan with her problems. It made her crazy to second guess herself.

A sudden thought popped into her head. There was someone she could go to. Someone who always fought her corner.

She was on her feet, keys in hand, before she could talk herself out of it. Twenty minutes later she pulled into the drive behind Veronica's sleek BMW. She turned off the engine and questioned the logic behind talking to Tyler's mother. It was easy to push the doubt aside because she was hers too, and had been since Veronica invited her into her home twenty years ago.

Still, she hesitated, waiting until the jumbled thoughts in her head settled. The door swung open a minute later, and Veronica stood under the silhouette of the porch light.

"Busted," Lilly-May said, climbing out of the car with a bright smile.

Veronica's eyes narrowed. "Hmm." She took Lilly-May by the hand. "What you need is some of my hot chocolate."

She laughed, despite the tightness in her chest. "I'd like to say things aren't that bad, but I could really use some right now."

Veronica guided her to the kitchen; the bright, happy colours seeping into her pores. It always felt like home.

"Take a seat. It won't take a minute."

She watched Veronica prepare her magic ingredients and couldn't help but think of the last time she'd tasted hot chocolate in this kitchen. Only it hadn't been Veronica at the stove, it had been Tyler.

The Davies had opened their doors on the day of her parents' funeral and taken care of all the details, including the wake. Lilly-May had barely functioned at the time, walking around in a daze. She had been grateful to hand over the reins.

The kicker had been meeting her father's mistress, who had arrived on Lilly-May's doorstep in floods of tears, two days after the accident. The woman had expected sympathy, had the gall to feign surprise when Lilly-May had kicked her to the curb.

She had been a zombie; putting one foot in front of the other because she had to. She hadn't cried, had refused to shed a tear for her father.

Tyler had found her inside the guest house, hiding from the well-wishers, and from her grief. He had put his arms around her without a word, holding her even when she got angry with him for forcing her to deal with the pain.

She had cried then, long and hard, and Tyler had been so patient. They had waited until the other guests left, and crept into the kitchen where Tyler had made her hot chocolate.

"Penny for them," Veronica said, placing a cup in front of her. It was piled high with marshmallows, so high there was a mini avalanche.

"I was just thinking about my parents' funeral, and Tyler making me one of these." Lilly-May scooped up the stray marshmallows and stuffed them into her mouth.

"I remember. He burnt the milk." Veronica smiled. "Only my Tyler could burn milk."

Tears sprang to Lilly-May's eyes. "Oh, V, I've made such a mess of things."

Veronica took both of her hands. "Talk to me, honey."

"It was hard, finding out my father was cheating on Mum. It made sense, the reason they were always fighting, I mean. But it hurt."

"Of course it did." Veronica looked towards the stove and back again. "I'm going to tell you something that's long overdue," she said, her tone solemn. "Your mum was ill for a long time, long before you were born."

Lilly-May ignored the wetness on her cheeks, holding onto Veronica's hands like a lifeline. "I've always known that. I think I knew even as a child, when a part of me thought it was my fault."

Veronica shook her head. "None of it was your fault, sweetheart."

"I know that too. But it doesn't excuse my father's behaviour."

"No. It doesn't." Veronica dropped a hand to reach forward and brush her fingers down Lilly-May's hair. "My point is, you have to stop blaming them. We all make mistakes, Lilly, but they loved you very much."

They sat in silence, Lilly-May deep in thought as she sipped her chocolate.

"I loved him so much. I looked up to him and it felt like a betrayal, not only to Mum, but to me too." Lilly-May studied her empty cup. "I've never given anyone else the chance to hurt me that way, yet today I hurt Tyler because of a ridiculous misunderstanding."

"Ah." Veronica sat back against the high-backed chair. "I have a feeling we might need something stronger."

Lilly-May smiled, soothed by the comfort, both in her stomach and in Veronica's presence. "Am I the only one who didn't know how he felt?"

Veronica dipped her head, pretending to consider the question. "Yes." She laughed easily. "When my boy loves, he loves deeply and for a long time he was happy you were part of the family. It was enough to be your friend."

"But it's not anymore?" Lilly-May knew the answer. She feared it.

"No. But that doesn't mean you can't adapt. He needed this, Lilly. He's been using Dylan as an excuse for far too long, and in your own way, so have you." Lilly-May didn't know how to respond so she remained quiet. "Not taking a chance," Veronica continued. "Is worse than taking a chance and failing. If you can't make it work, maybe he can finally move on."

"Are you angry with me?" she whispered, holding Veronica's quiet gaze.

"Of course not, sweetheart. Whatever brought you to my door, I know you would never hurt him intentionally." She got up and walked around the counter. "You'll figure it out, Lilly." She wrapped her arms around her. "And I'll be here for you each step of the way."

It was all she needed to hear. "I'm so confused, V. I've loved him most of my life, but I sometimes feel like we're strangers."

Veronica kissed the top of her head. "Perhaps you always knew what would happen if you let him in. What you have to ask yourself is, was it fear of commitment that kept you at arm's length, or that your heart already belonged to another?"

Lilly-May closed her eyes. "One way or the other I'll fix things. I can't bear to think that I might have ruined everything."

"You just have to talk to him," Veronica said, with a gentle squeeze. "If you're honest with each other, things will start to make sense."

She hoped Veronica was right because Tyler was hurting, and if she risked everything to heal that hurt, it would destroy them both if she got it wrong.

Chapter 12

Lilly-May went straight to Tyler's when she left his parents' house, but he wasn't home. She tried ringing, even left a voicemail, and was sorely tempted to search his regular hangouts. In the end she went home because they both needed space.

It didn't help her sleep. She tossed and turned until 4am, before getting up to put her restless energy to good use.

She arrived at the café just before 5am, ready to cook up a storm. The silence set her on edge as soon as she walked in. It felt wrong. She couldn't put her finger on it, she just knew something wasn't right.

It wasn't until she was half-way across the room that it clicked into place. There was someone else in the building, and more to the point there was somebody upstairs. Every hair on the back of her neck stood up. She felt rooted to the spot by indecision. Her instincts told her to get out and fast, yet a part of her didn't want to leave her cafe in the hands of an intruder. Who knew what they were doing up there. It took seconds to make her decision. She was across the room and in the kitchen before she could change her mind; flipping the bolt across the door.

She pulled out her phone and rang Tyler without thinking, desperate to hear his voice.

"Hello?" came the sleepy reply.

"Ty, I'm at the café and I'm not alone."

She heard the sound of sheets ruffling. "What do you mean you're not alone?"

"I mean someone is upstairs and I'm locked in the kitchen wondering what to do about it."

"You get the hell out of there, that's what you do about it." He paused. "Are you sure it's not a member of staff? What about the alarm?"

She considered that. "The alarm was on, so if my staff were camping out here without my knowledge, I think they would have thought of that."

"Shit."

She heard more rustling.

"I'm on my way. Get out of there, Lilly and call the police."

"You're right. I'll do that." She dashed across the kitchen to the exit, fumbling for her keys. The wave of relief crashed at her feet when the door hit something solid on the other side. She couldn't even get her hand through the gap. "Something's blocking the exit," she said, turning to head back the other way. She froze when she heard footsteps on the stairs. "They're coming," she croaked into the phone, ducking behind the large preparation counter.

Tyler's response was a little out of breath, like he was running. "I'm coming," he said, not hiding his panic. "Don't open the door until I get there."

She almost screamed when the door knob rattled. A moment later she heard something much worse, and knew what it was before she caught the smell. "Ty, you might want to hurry. I smell kerosene."

"Shit."

She heard an engine roar.

"I need to call it in. Get out of there, Lilly. Now."

"Okay." She fumbled with the phone, but her fingers shook so violently it dropped to the floor.

Stupid. Stupid. Stupid.

"Get a hold of yourself," she whispered, then glanced nervously at the door. She could hear someone moving on the other side.

She turned and began to crawl towards the small window.

Stupid.

She was supposed to be calling the police. Rising to her feet, since the intruder made no attempt to break through the door, she walked to retrieve the phone. It rang before she reached it, catching her by surprise. This time she couldn't hold back the squeak, even though she had a hand clamped over her mouth.

Bringing the offending article to her ear, she almost wept when she heard Sebastian's voice.

"Lilly, are you safe?" he asked, his usual restraint slipping. "Did you get out?"

"Not yet. I forgot my phone." She started backing towards the window.

"The police are on their way. Just get out, Lilly. Dylan and I will be there in fifteen minutes."

"Thank you." She glanced at the window, at the narrow opening, and at the rolling-pin laying on the drainer. "And I'm sorry," she said, grabbing the tool and aiming it at the glass. She didn't catch Sebastian's response. She was too busy ridding the frame of every shard.

"Hang on a minute," she said, tucking the phone in her back pocket.

She was half-way through the window when she heard a loud explosion and lost her footing. Luckily she didn't have far to fall, but it still hurt when she hit the ground.

With a low groan she scraped herself off the pavement and glanced to her left, frowning when she saw the pick-up truck. She ignored the trickle of unease and turned right, creeping to the corner of the building. The welcome sound of an approaching fire engine gave her a boost.

Still, she was cautious, peering around the corner to take in the scene at the front of the café. It took her a second to understand. There was a tall, thin male, lying on the ground in front of the long bank of windows. Glass littered the pavement around the man, peppered with what looked like blood. She saw flames reaching towards the early morning light, seeking something – what she wasn't entirely sure.

Creeping forward, she sucked in a breath the moment she felt the heat. It was intense. Her gaze dropped to the man on the ground, then shot to the flashing lights of an approaching fire engine. She crept closer, trying to distance herself from the incredible heat of the fire. She didn't look inside the café. She knew she would fall apart if she saw the room burning.

Up close she saw the man was badly injured. There was blood seeping onto the ground beneath his head, so though she knew she shouldn't move him, she was caught between a rock and a hard place. If she'd didn't he would burn. He was the reason the flames were trying to climb outside. She could smell the fuel on his clothes.

Grabbing his jacket she turned her face away and pulled with all her might. It was like pulling a barge, though the sweat dripping down her face had more to do with the heat than exertion.

"Lilly?"

She turned toward the sound of her name. Steve, one of Tyler's colleagues, rushed forward, mask in hand.

She released the man's jacket, stumbling in her relief. "I can't move him. I think he was blown through the window."

Steve took her elbow, signalling to his crew as he led her across the street. "It's okay, Lilly. Let us take care of this." He searched her face. "How long were you inside?"

She shook her head, knowing what he was asking. "I got out through the kitchen window. I wasn't anywhere near the fire. At least not until...Oh god. I was so stupid."

"You're going to be fine," he said, glancing towards his crew. "I'll be right back, okay?"

"Yes. Go. You have a job to do."

She didn't watch him cross the street, she still couldn't look at the café. Her legs gave out just thinking about the destruction the fire had already caused. The phone, still in her back pocket, hit the pavement with a thud.

"Crap. Sebastian!" she squeaked, retrieving the surprisingly undamaged phone.

The moment she heard Sebastian's voice in her ear she burst into tears, and didn't stop until he arrived seven and a half minutes later.

***

Tyler had never been so afraid. Driving towards Café 101 was like a journey into the past. The image of the bright yellow Beetle, Lilly's first car, flashed into his head over and over. Only this time he knew the situation was much worse because Lilly was in danger.

He almost lost it when he saw the damage at the café. He couldn't even get out of the car, he was so afraid of what he would find. But, like the answer to his prayers, Sebastian stepped up to his door.

"She's fine, Ty. She's with Dylan in his SUV." He nodded to the other side of the street, at a safe distance from the danger zone.

Tyler was beside his brother a heartbeat later. "I'm sorry about the café, Seb. Shit, if this is the son of a bitch who-"

Sebastian put a hand on his shoulder. "The ambulance just left with the arsonist. From what I can gather he panicked when he realised somebody was inside and he'd made a mistake."

"Son of a bitch. He could have killed her." The thought made him sick. "Give me a minute and I'll go find out what's going on." He crossed to the SUV first to reassure himself Lilly was okay. She was asleep against Dylan's shoulder, the after effects of adrenalin and a sleepless night. Her cheeks were red, like she'd gotten a little too close to the fire, but she was safe. It was all that mattered.

Nodding to Dylan he moved on, passing the police car because he knew it was empty without looking. He could see two officers talking to Mike, their Watch Manager, while his colleagues battled the fire.

It was hard to be an observer when it was his job to fight alongside his friends. Even knowing he was too close to this one, it didn't help to calm the jitters. He wanted to suit up.

Mike inclined his head when Tyler stepped up to the group, but didn't stop talking. "As soon as we get inside we'll be able to confirm our suspicions. We'll also be able to ascertain if this is the work of the same guy."

"It's him," Tyler cut in. "It's not a coincidence that the Davies name was all over the local news and then one of my brother's properties gets targeted."

"This is Tyler Davies," Mike said. "He's one of ours. His brother owns Café 101 with Miss Saunders."

Officer Emily Bishop removed her cap, nodding at him from beneath a thick mop of curls. "Tyler and I go way back." She held out a hand, which he took.

"How did he get in?" he asked, thinking about the alarm again. It was state of the art.

"We found a pick-up truck parked around back," Emily said, after glancing at her partner. "It appears he climbed onto the cab and used the balcony as the point of entry."

Tyler frowned. "Any idea how he bypassed the alarm?"

"It appears to have been tampered with, but we have a representative from the company on their way. Miss Saunders remembers disengaging the alarm when she entered the property, so it's not clear at this point."

Tyler glanced toward the building, watching the team battle back the fire with a ferocity which made him proud. The need to jump in was a prickle along his skin.

"There's nothing you can do here right now," Mike said, understanding. "Why don't you take care of your family and I'll update you as soon as I have anything."

"Okay." Tyler nodded to Emily, then her partner. "I won't be far."

Lilly-May was awake when he got back to Dylan's SUV. His brothers were on either side of her on the backseat so he climbed into the front.

He met her eyes, saw the fatigue and the uncertainty. "How are you doing?" he asked, wishing he could reach out to her.

"I'm feeling pretty stupid, especially the part where I locked myself in a building with an intruder."

Dylan put his arm around her. "Not to mention pulling said intruder out of the path of fire," he grumbled.

Lilly-May's gaze never left Tyler's. She didn't say anything else for the longest time. "I guess you never really know what you'll do in a crisis. I can't believe you do this all the time" she said, looking out onto the street. After a second or two her eyes locked with his again. "That you want to be out there right now."

"Of course he does. Those guys out there, they're his family too."

Tyler turned to Sebastian with a smile. "They have it covered." He looked away. "I'm just sorry this happened because they got a hold of my name."

Sebastian shook his head. "It's not your fault, Ty."

"No, it's not," Dylan agreed. "And we can rebuild. At least nobody got hurt."

They all flinched when someone tapped against the window. Tyler turned with the sound of Lilly's nervous laughter echoing around them.

Mike signalled from the other side of the glass, then walked towards the truck. Tyler got out and followed.

His father was just pulling into a vacant spot opposite. He climbed out of the car with a large basket of supplies. Tyler would have bet money on his mother's hot chocolate being in there, along with a few cookies. He would get in on the action as soon as he got back.

"Good to see you, Dad," he said, pausing to slap a hand on his shoulder.

"Your mother drove to Addy's so she can watch Elijah. Adrienne wants to be here too."

Tyler grinned, moving forward after a light squeeze of his father's shoulder. The Davies family always rallied, and pretty soon they would have more help than they could handle, considering the extended family.

He glanced back briefly, caught Lilly watching him from the SUV and felt his heart settle. They would get through this.

***

Lilly-May opened her eyes to a wall of black, only to realise she'd buried herself beneath the covers. She hadn't made it home until 5pm, so after the questions, the tears, the waiting and the sleepless night, she had fallen into bed intending to grab a few hours. Instead she had slept right through until – her eyes grew huge when she focused on her digital clock. It was 9am, which meant she had slept for sixteen hours.

"What the-" She snatched up her phone when it shrilled on her nightstand. "Yeah. Hello?"

"Lilly. Thank god," Adrienne said. "I've been calling you for hours."

Her eyes fell to her mobile on the side. "My battery is dead. What's going on?" Lilly-May heard a rush of breath a moment before Adrienne began speaking a mile a minute.

"You won't believe how many people have called the station this morning offering support. Resources, time, money, I can't keep track of them all. It's wonderful, Lilly."

"The Davies family do a lot for the city," she said, fighting back a rush of emotion.

"I know, but this is unbelievable." She paused. "Anyway, I'm between tracks so I'd better get on with it. Can you meet me at the restaurant around noon?"

"Of course." She expected they had a lot to talk about.

"I have a surprise for you," Adrienne continued. "Or rather, Sebastian, Chris and Dylan have a surprise, but it was my idea." Another pause. "Trust me, you'll love it. See you then."

Lilly-May stared at the phone, wishing she could drum up some of Addy's enthusiasm. Maybe she'd slept too long, she thought, heaving her lazy butt out of bed.

She was just dragging on a pair of jeans when the doorbell sounded. Fastening the buttons as she crossed the room, she grabbed a t-shirt from a drawer. The buzzer sounded again when she stepped into the hall, then a third and a fourth time in quick succession.

"Okay. I'm coming," she called, jogging down the steps.

Her heart sped up the moment she saw Tyler. His piercing blue eyes searched her face. "I've been calling," he said, sounding relieved. "I left messages."

Lilly-May pulled a face, stepping back to let him in. "I was comatose."

There was a brief, awkward silence, while Tyler paced the entry hall. "I just need to get this out," he said, running a hand through his hair. From the thick grooves it was obvious he'd been doing that a lot. "I'm sorry, Lilly. And I want you to know that I meant what I said before. What happened between us won't ruin anything. We're still family."

"Nice speech." She waited until he looked at her. "Why does it sound like you're giving up?"

Tyler stepped forward, his eyes searching again. "I thought that's what you wanted?"

"Maybe," she said, taking a step of her own. "It just takes me longer to catch up."

His eyes narrowed. "What are you saying?"

"I'm saying I was confused, afraid even, but I certainly don't want to throw in the towel." She closed the distance, taking his hand to lead him to the couch.

"We had an argument, Ty, and I'm sorry I hurt you." She ran her free hand through the grooves in his hair. "In some ways it was a good thing, because it forced things out in the open."

Tyler raised his brows. "I was keeping a pretty big secret," he smile was full of boyish charm. "I thought it would scare you away."

"That a strong, passionate, sexy man loves me. Why would it scare me away?" Lilly-May laughed when his brows rose a second time. "*Oh,*" she exaggerated the word, watching humour light his eyes. "You're referring to the whole commitment issue." She leant closer, lowering her voice to a whisper. "You used the L word."

"You know what I mean," he said laughing. "Jamie said I went from 0 to 60 in a heartbeat – without giving you a chance to catch up."

Lilly-May bit her lip. "Says the man who only has one gear." Her brow creased. "That made more sense in my head!"

"If I'd told you in the beginning," Tyler said, wrinkling his nose. "Used the L word. We wouldn't be having this conversation." He tilted his head. "Do you remember what you asked me that day, when you were trying to process the kiss?"

She nodded, picturing the confrontation. "I asked you where it came from."

"And I lied. I told you I didn't know," he glanced at their joined hands. "It felt safer than the truth. That I've loved you my whole life."

Lilly-May felt tears burn her eyes. "You're right, that would have terrified me. But I think it would still have led us here. I wasn't lying when I said you awoke something in me, Ty, and it isn't about the physical."

"No?" He placed a fingertip on her chin, running it down the centre of her body in a slow, torturous journey that made her stomach muscles clench in anticipation. "Are you sure about that?"

"Okay," she murmured, struggling to catch her breath. "That still takes me by surprise. You only have to look at me," her eyes widened, "like you're doing right now, and I want you."

He leant forward, releasing her hand so he could thread his fingers into her hair. "I can get on board with that."

Lilly-May swallowed the groan building in her throat and shook her head. "Stop distracting me. I'm serious. I'm trying to tell you that it's not about the chemistry, that I-"

Tyler silenced her with a kiss, though it was fleeting and held an edge of desperation. "Don't say it, if it's not a hundred percent truth," he said, touching his forehead to hers. "I can wait, Lilly. If this is what you want, I'll wait."

She wrapped her arms around him, her brain searching for a way to make him understand. Energy buzzed along her skin, the restless kind she had never been able to control. "I need you to listen to me. Can you do that?" she asked, sitting back. He opened his mouth to speak, but she shook her head. "I mean it, Ty. No interruptions until I've finished."

The moment he inclined his head she sprang to her feet. "I've been thinking a lot about relationships in the past couple of days and, before, when I said our fight was a good thing, I meant it." She had to pace a little, it helped to focus her thoughts. "I needed to put things in perspective."

Her gaze shot to his, saw the nerves in his eyes. For some reason, it calmed the restless feeling inside her. "You know how I felt about my parents, and how much I struggled because of my father's betrayal. I used to think it was the reason I protected my heart so fiercely. It was easier to love my friends and family, and to keep a part of myself back."

Tyler stood to face her, but he didn't speak so she rushed on.

"It took seeing you with Lorna to realise my mistake. I'm not going to tell you I wasn't jealous, because seeing you with another woman was-"

"You don't have to do this, Lilly," Tyler said, voice thick with emotion.

She narrowed her eyes at him. "Yes I do."

His proximity was making it harder to think. "The fact is, I was momentarily blinded by that jealously because, imagining you with someone else - that wasn't what really scared me." She moved closer, giving in to the need. "The thought of losing you finally helped me to understand that I wasn't protecting my heart at all, in fact, I had already given it away."

"Lilly."

She understood the quiet plea. He wanted to believe her, but he was afraid.

"It belongs to you, Tyler," she said, taking both his hands. "My heart belongs to you." This time when she felt the tears burn, she let them fall. "Every time the Davies boys came to the café, or there was a family event, or an impromptu get together, it was you I looked forward to seeing. You I trusted to keep things in order, or to say the right thing. I think that part of me didn't want to analyse those feelings. The joy of having you in my life felt too precious to ruin it with complications."

She saw that he understood, and that her words were finally sinking in.

"What a fool I've been," he whispered. "So much time wasted." He captured her face in his hands. "I've loved you for so long, Lilly, that it blinded me too. If I had allowed myself to dream, to hope you might feel the same..." He shook his head.

"Tell me," she demanded, meeting his intense gaze. "I want to hear you say it."

Tyler bent to capture her mouth, his lips gentle, coaxing – almost reverent. "I love you." It was a whisper against her mouth. "I've loved you since the day you first put your hand in mine." He reached for her hand and brought it to his lips. "I will always love you."

Lilly-May launched herself at him, the swell of emotion so strong she had no choice but to ride it. "Thank god. The thought of not being able to touch you…I want to touch you, Tyler."

He laughed against her mouth. "I'm not stopping you."

"Promise me something," she said, her hands impatient in their exploration.

"Uh, uh," Tyler shook his head. "There's no going back now." He sucked in a breath when Lilly-May found his flesh, her fingers flittering across his skin.

"No," she said, between kisses. "I want you to promise me there's no more hiding, no more secrets."

His hand slid to cup the back of her neck, stilling her. "Lilly, I want everyone to know that you're mine. I couldn't possible hide that."

"I love it when you say things like that," she whispered, eyes burning. "I love how you make me feel."

He tempered her quiet desperation with a kiss. It soothed as much as it burned, and she melted in his arms.

Chapter 13

Tyler glanced across at Lilly-May, part of him still waiting for the other shoe to drop. Every moment they'd shared over the last twenty years was playing on a loop in his head; his brain searching for the clues they had missed. The lingering looks, the silences, the way she would smile when he entered the room. It hadn't been the brotherly affection she shared with Dylan, or the bond she had with Sebastian.

He couldn't help thinking about all the time he'd wasted, all the excuses he'd made to himself and his family.

"Did they tell you about the surprise," Lilly asked, shaking him out of his reverie.

"No. Whatever it is, they didn't share it with me." He took his eyes from the road briefly. "And we both know I'm good at keeping secrets."

Lilly-May laughed, placing a hand on his thigh.

His foot jerked against the accelerator. "Maybe we should have some rules about the touching," he said, clearing his throat.

"What?" she asked in a deceptively innocent voice. "Is this distracting?" Her hand slid up a few inches.

"Lilly."

He turned to see her eyes laughing back at him. It was tempting to pull over and play a little. The smile dropped from her lips so fast his heart stuttered.

"Thank you," she whispered, moving her hand to grip his on the steering wheel.

"For what?"

"For turning my world upside down."

He swallowed hard. "You turned my world upside down the moment my father found you asleep under the stars."

"It scared me half to death when I saw him crouching above me."

He could tell she was smiling. He could hear it in her voice. "I think you scared him too. I've never seen him quite so unsure of himself."

"You're a lot like him, you know," she said, threading her fingers through his. "The protectors of the family."

He didn't know what to do with that. When it came to Lilly-May, being the responsible one had always felt like a bad thing.

It turned out he didn't get the chance to respond because, when they pulled into Main Street, they saw Lilly's surprise in all its glory. A big, bold catering truck, equipped with the Café 101 logo.

"How did he pull this off so quickly?" Tyler wondered aloud.

He had barely pulled to the curb when Lilly leapt from her seat and ran towards the group outside Winchesters.

Chris swept her off her feet and spun her in a wide circle. "Is that not the sweetest machine you've ever seen in your life?"

Tyler watched her face light up, and thought her smile was by far the sweetest.

She went down the line, her enthusiasm bubbling over. "You guys are the best," she said, hugging Dylan. "I may have to take my show on the road with this baby."

"Now there's an idea." Tyler stepped forward to shake Chris' hand.

Lilly-May took it before Chris could, yanking Tyler down for a kiss that had the others whooping.

"Oh come on," Lilly said, without turning. "Like you didn't know this was going to happen."

"He took his sweet time about it," Dylan said, winking at his brother. "I thought I was going to have to light a fire under his ass."

"Ha. Ha." Tyler hooked an arm around Lilly's shoulders. "How long have you been saving that one?"

Dylan wiggled his brows, enjoying himself far too much. "My point exactly, brother. My point exactly."

"Speaking of fires," Adrienne said, unlocking the beast on wheels. "Do you have any news?"

"Not yet. The team are still combing through the building. But it's not hard to guess what their findings will be." Tyler shook his head.

"At least we have an explanation for the alarm," Sebastian cut in, holding out a hand to Lilly-May. "The arsonist managed to disable it, but the system malfunctioned and the ground floor remained active."

"I've said for a while that we need an upgrade. The unit wasn't modified when we extended." This came from Chris, who had clambered into the food van ahead of the others. "The question is – how are we going to secure this beauty?"

Tyler stood back to watch his family explore the new toy. Adrienne hung back with him, linking her arm through his, and resting her head on his shoulder.

"I'm so happy for you, Ty," she whispered.

"Thanks, sister mine." He kissed the top of her head. "How's Lucy?"

"Scared," she admitted. "But we'll get through it."

"We'll make sure that you do."

They stood, amused by the bickering coming from the van, yet drawing strength, as they had always done – from family.

***

"I have a surprise of my own," Tyler told Lilly-May as they finished dinner later that evening. "I realised how fortunate we are, not because of the family name, or the money, but because we have a strong foundation."

She put down the plate she was about to clear away, stepping over to sit in his lap. "I'm guessing I should be sitting down for this."

He grinned, touching his forehead to hers. "I bought Rutherford Towers, or the site anyway. Dylan is going to help me build a Community Shelter, and I'm going to put Grayson's name on it."

Lilly-May cupped his face in her hands, leaning to place a kiss to his lips. "That's what I love about you, Tyler. You never let things go."

He felt warmth flash through his body. "You love me, huh?"

"Like fire loves oxygen."

He rubbed his nose against hers. "I can live with that comparison."

"Hmm," she whispered, raining kisses along his jaw. "I've got a lot to learn about this obsession of yours." Her eyes danced when they met his. "Want to whisper fire codes in my ear?"

He tucked his hands beneath her legs and stood. "I think I can do better than that," he said, kissing her. He'd been waiting far too long to share the fire in his heart.

Printed in Great Britain
by Amazon.co.uk, Ltd.,
Marston Gate.